She tried to remember where she had seen him before, but she couldn't place him. She thought she knew everyone around here, so he must be new.

"*Jambo*, Miss Butler," he held out his hand and smiled timidly at Hannah. She shook his hand.

"I'm sorry; have we met before?" she answered.

"Oh, please forgive me for not introducing myself." The man flushed, turning nearly the color of his red hair. "I'm Dan Williams. I am the teacher at the mission school over by Limara." Hannah smiled and thought how different he was from Garth. Garth would never look so flustered and awkward at the mere prospect of introducing himself.

"What is it I can do for you this morning, Mr. Williams? Or should I call you Reverend Williams?" Hannah found herself replying to him confidently and professionally, the way she would have liked to be able to speak to Garth.

"Oh, my, no!" He blushed and looked down at his dusty boots. "I'm just a teacher. It's that one of my students, you see. . ." He stopped and looked around.

"Mr. Williams!" Hannah spoke quickly, suddenly embarrassed for him. "I'm a vet. Not a doctor. I don't treat students."

"Oh, my goodness, how silly of me. It's not the student I want you to look at; I didn't mean that at all. It's that the student brought me an animal, an elephant, actually. It's the elephant, Miss Butler."

SALLY KRUEGER has seen much of the world. She was born in England and lived in Kenya as a child. She wrote her first published novel, *The Promise of Rain,* while living in Scotland for a short time. Sally currently lives with her husband and four children in Alberta, Canada.

Books by Sally Krueger

HEARTSONG PRESENTS
HP256—The Promise of Rain

Don't miss out on any of our super romances. Write to us at the following address for information on our newest releases and club information.

Heartsong Presents Readers' Service
PO Box 719
Uhrichsville, OH 44683

Some Trust in Horses

Sally Krueger

Heartsong Presents

To my daughter,
Caitlin, who loves animals,
with all my love.

A note from the author:
I love to hear from my readers! You may correspond with me by writing:

Sally Krueger
Author Relations
PO Box 719
Uhrichsville, OH 44683

ISBN 1-57748-633-1

SOME TRUST IN HORSES

Cover illustration by Jocelyne Bouchard.

PRINTED IN THE U.S.A.

one

The little foal struggled to stand up, fighting as much against its own gangly legs as against gravity. Hannah breathed a sigh of relief. The foal wasn't breathing properly when it was born that morning, and by the time Garth, its owner, had found Hannah, the foal was almost gone. Hannah had quickly pulled her suction equipment out of her saddlebags, found the clogged mucous, and dislodged it.

"Thanks, Han, old chap! I really don't know what I'd do without you."

Hannah looked up into Garth's handsome, smiling face. She smiled back quickly and started packing up her equipment. She always felt awkward with Garth, and she wanted to make her getaway before he started teasing her. He seemed to think it was hugely funny that a woman should be a vet, and she was easy prey because she was always too tongue-tied and shy with him to fire back some witty comment and deflect her embarrassment. She used to think she preferred the company of animals to people, but Garth was making her feel that it was merely that she was less afraid of animals than of people.

Hannah threw the bags over the rump of her horse, Kindye, and turned around to say good-bye. Garth was pulling some bills out of his pocket. Her fee. She reached out and took it.

"Thanks, Mr. Whitehead." She pulled her hat out of the back pocket of her trousers, stuffed the money in, and plastered her hat over her frizzy blond thatch of hair.

5

"How many times do I have to tell you, Han, old chap, call me Garth. Until I get the hang of raising horses in this African veldt, you and I will be seeing a lot of each other. If the tsetse flies or the lions or the snakes don't get them, the heat or the diseases will! That is, unless you help me out!"

Hannah could feel it coming. She turned and mounted Kindye and whistled for Simba, her dog. The big golden lab came bounding out good-naturedly from behind the stables. Garth continued.

"Not that I mind, of course. Working with a woman vet is a rare treat, even if she does wear trousers and the ugliest hat I've ever seen. I'd hire you, Han, even if you weren't the only vet within a hundred miles." He laughed delightedly at his little joke. Hannah knew that every unmarried woman in Kikuru would give her eyeteeth to be laughing with the rich, blue-eyed horse breeder and racer, but she couldn't wait to get away.

She ducked her head and tried to smile back. "I have another call to make before lunch," she lied. Giving Kindye a slight nudge with her heel, she trotted quickly down the jacaranda-lined driveway and out onto the dusty road that led into town.

Out on the road, Hannah slowed Kindye to a walk. She was in no rush to get home to Mother. The heat of the African noon made the dust in the air shimmer and shine, but there was a telltale breeze. Hannah looked upward just as a huge black cloud covered the sun. Suddenly, she could hear the rain thundering behind her, galloping like the giant herds of wildebeest out on the plains, swooping down onto her from over the hill that stood behind Garth's farm. She urged Kindye into a gallop to reach the nearest thorn tree beside the road. The tabletop branches were thin, thorny, and almost useless as shelter from the rain, but she and the animals waited anyway.

Peering through the torrent, Hannah could already see that sunshine was swallowing up the tail of the storm. Steam rose off the dusty grassland in its wake, sucked upwards into the blue sky. Soon the sunshine reached Hannah's thorn tree, but the rain still fell. *A monkey's wedding,* thought Hannah, remembering the old expression her father had used, and how she and her father would race out of the house to be part of the wedding. Hannah had always looked up into the tall trees that surrounded their house to see if she could see the monkeys getting married. Her father laughed and said, "One day, Han, one day!"

But the years since he had died had slowed and stretched out, long and cheerless. Even taking over his practice hadn't really helped the pain in the way she had hoped it would. But over the years the aching void he had left in her heart had crusted over and left a scar. Maybe it was because of Mother. But that was another story. Hannah shook her head. Time to be getting on. She whistled for Simba and they stepped out into the road, which was now a torrent of red, steaming, muddy water.

Up ahead, a clutch of little totos played and splashed in the stream, and quickly their black skins turned as red as the mud they played in. Their mothers, walking along the road with baskets of vegetables on their heads, laughed and chattered together, enjoying the brief reprieve from the heat and dust.

"*Jambo,* memsahib," they chorused as Hannah rode past. She smiled down at them and envied them for their easy, friendly ways, and their children and their homes. What she wouldn't give for that. But the only hope she had of marriage was, as her mother never failed to make abundantly clear, with Charles Montague. She shuddered. Not that he wouldn't be a good catch and a good husband, in his own way, but she just couldn't bring herself to encourage him. And he would insist she give up her practice and join the proper social circles. How much of herself would she be willing to sacrifice for marriage? And why did getting married have to be such an unpleasant business? She had always dreamed and read that it was a wonderful and romantic experience, not merely the least of several unhappy alternatives.

Hannah sighed. She was twenty-five years old this year. Mother was getting very difficult to put off much longer. She was practically courting Charles for her. She would have to make up her mind soon. It was too bad that Charles couldn't be more like Garth. The thought caught Hannah by surprise. Garth always made her feel like running away, but something about him made her think about him on the lonely evenings and long rides through the countryside. She never gave Charles a thought if she could help it.

She rode alone along the outskirts of Kikuru, where she and her mother lived in a lovely Spanish-style house with a red tile roof and a courtyard in the center. She turned into a tree-lined driveway with an old worn sign that Hannah no longer saw. "Dr. Butler's Veterinary Clinic," it read. Her father had been Dr. Butler and had built the clinic at the corner where the driveway and the road met. Hannah rode past the neat concrete building with the corrugated iron roof glinting in the midday sun. The house was just visible through a bushy forest of brush that sheltered it from the road.

As Hannah came through the trees, she glimpsed her mother waiting for her, as usual, on the veranda where they always took their lunch. But today there was someone else there too. Hannah's heart sank. Surely it couldn't be Charles Montague. Mother hadn't said anything about him coming for lunch. But as Hannah rode a little closer, she realized it was indeed Charles. Simba suddenly noticed him too and ran up onto the veranda barking and growling. Simba had never liked Charles, and no matter how many times he came to visit, she always barked at him as if she had never seen him before. Unkindly, Hannah hesitated before calling her back. Poor Charles, try as he might, could never quite disguise his fear of large dogs. He stood up quickly and put his chair between himself and Simba. Reluctantly, Hannah called her.

"Simba, Simba, come!" Simba turned slowly around, giving one last growl over her shoulder before returning to where Hannah was just dismounting and handing Kindye over to the syce to take to the stable.

"Hannah Butler!" Mrs. Butler's shrill voice accosted Hannah as she started up the stairs of the veranda. "What have you been doing? You're dripping wet! Charles has been so good to pay us a call and you turn up looking like something the cat dragged in. It is bad enough you insisting on dressing like a shenzi old farmer, but you're soaked to the skin! Go and change at once!"

"Mother, I got caught in the downpour. It couldn't be helped. Hello, Charles. If you'll excuse me for a moment. Simba, stay!"

"Well, hurry up! Juma has the food ready and it's getting cold."

Hannah shot Charles a grim smile as she walked around the table to the door. Simba lay down, careful to keep one eye cocked open in case Charles moved. To her disappointment, he only sat gingerly back down and kept one eye on her as well.

Hannah suddenly felt tired. She really didn't feel like having lunch with Charles. He probably wanted to invite her to some profoundly dull function at the Kikuru Club and she would have to turn him down, then she would have to face her mother's fury. Maybe it would just be easier to accept whatever invitation he was going to spring on her. She sighed. No, that would only encourage him to invite her again. She changed into a clean white shirt and new pair of khaki trousers. She knew her mother would be expecting her to be in a dress, but she had work to do after lunch.

Charles Montague always had this disquieting effect on her. Whenever she gave him any thought, she could only conclude that he was a very nice person, and she should be pleased that he took an interest in her. But when she was actually in his presence, she had the most perverse inclination not to have anything to do with him. She could barely muster enough civility to turn him down politely. She just didn't understand what came over her. Surely every woman didn't go through this kind of conflict when a man invited her to go somewhere with him. She had never read about it in any books. She didn't really know anyone she could ask such a personal question of, either. The closest person she had to a friend was Fiona Brown, but she wouldn't really be able to ask her about that sort of thing.

Hannah finished dragging a comb through her damp hair. It didn't take very long. Her hair was short and just sprang back into its usual unruly yellow curls the minute the comb let it go. Hannah glanced at herself in the mirror, shrugged, and headed out to the veranda.

As she opened the door, Charles eagerly sprang up to pull out her chair for her. Simba immediately sat up and growled.

"Down, Simba. Thank you, Charles," said Hannah, feeling her mother's disapproving glare on her clothes.

Juma followed Hannah onto the veranda with a tray of steaming platters. Hannah had tried for years to persuade her mother to serve something cold for lunch on such hot, muggy days, but she may as well have tried to move a mountain.

Mrs. Butler's routines, of which a hot luncheon was the centerpiece, were her bulwark against the uncivilizing effects of Africa on her family. The further Hannah strayed from conventional womanly behavior, the more strictly Mrs. Butler's routines were enforced.

Everyone helped themselves to slices of tender roast beef and mounds of creamy mashed potatoes, then poured hot, thick gravy over them. Vegetables consisted of peas and carrots dripping with dollops of melted butter. In the heat of the African midday, it was ridiculous. It put her in a bad mood. She decided to take the bull by the horns and find out what Charles had come for.

"Well, Charles, it's lovely to have such an unexpected visit from you," she began, sounding as buttery as the peas. "What brings you out this way?"

Unfortunately, poor Charles had just taken a bite of beef. Hannah smiled sweetly and watched him swallow it almost whole before answering. He was a tall, pale man with a long face and a very upper-class beak of a nose. He had long arms with long, delicate fingers. Hannah thought he would have looked perfectly at home eating roast beef and drinking brandy in a club in London, rather than out here in the fierce sunlight and rough-and-tumble of the African colonies. But, he was, like Garth Whitehead, a younger son, and had been sent out to make his fortune in Africa. He was working for the British government as a district commissioner, and Hannah predicted he would soon be able to go home and find work in the civil service in England, where he would live happily ever after telling stories of grand adventures in darkest Africa to his grandchildren.

He cleared his throat and looked pleadingly at Hannah from under his long, pale eyelashes. "Miss Butler. Hannah." Hannah, unkindly, didn't respond. He carried on anyway.

"I know you are interested in the horse races and Garth Whitehead—you know him, don't you?" Hannah nodded, suddenly interested. "Well, Garth has reserved a box at the Kikuru Cup Races in two weeks, and he's invited a group of us to join him watching his horses race from the box with him. I would like to invite you to join me in Garth's box, as my guest." He stopped speaking and waited for Hannah's reply.

Hannah found herself involuntarily smiling at him as she paused with a forkful of vegetables halfway up to her mouth. "Why, Mr. Montague, that sounds very nice. I'd love to watch the races with you from Mr. Whitehead's box. How nice of you to think of inviting me." Hannah popped her food into her mouth and felt as shocked with herself for accepting as Charles did that she had accepted.

Mrs. Butler was ecstatic. "What a grand plan! I'm so thrilled you've invited Hannah to go with you. And in Mr. Whitehead's box too. Aren't you thrilled, Hannah? I'm going with the Fitzhughs myself. It is going to be such an exciting day. Everyone who is anyone will be there, don't you know, Hannah?"

Hannah already regretted accepting Charles's invitation, but she couldn't figure out what on earth had possessed her to do so. Now she had two weeks of her mother's planning and scheming to look forward to, and surely that was far worse than her temper when Hannah insisted on saying no to Charles.

"But I only have one small request, Mr. Montague—"

"Hannah, you must call me Charles. I insist upon it!"

"Alright then, Charles, there is just one thing I must ask. I am obligated to look in on Mr. Whitehead's horses before the races. I need to be sure that they are all in good running condition, so if you don't mind, I'll have to meet you there."

"No, not at all. That will—"

"Hannah! You can't be serious!" Mrs. Butler's voice pierced the conversation like a machete. "You can't possibly mean that you are going to work, and in a filthy stable, no less, when you have been invited to watch the races in a box with Charles Montague. I won't allow it; I simply will not!"

"Oh, it really is alright with me, Mrs.—" Poor Charles gallantly tried to come to her rescue, but Mrs. Butler cut him off.

"It is most certainly not alright! She will smell like a horse! And how on earth will she wear the right clothes if she has to go traipsing around a stable checking the undersides of sweaty horses like some common syce. I won't have it, Hannah Butler; I won't." Mrs. Butler's voice was like the high-pitched whistle of the train. Charles was turning pink with embarrassment at the scene he had inadvertently caused. Hannah was livid.

"Mother! How dare you speak to me this way in front of Mr. Mon—I mean—Charles. Stop it. Now." Hannah hissed the command between her teeth, and her mother was so taken aback by her daughter's fury she stopped herself just as she was about to let another barrage go.

"We'll discuss this later," Hannah said, glaring her down and then smiling grimly at Charles. "Thank you very much for inviting me. Now, let's see," she searched desperately for another topic. "Have you heard any news from Europe lately? I hear there is quite a bit of talk of war. I don't believe it will actually come to that, do you, Charles?"

Charles looked immensely relieved, "Yes, some people are saying that a war is inevitable. The Balkans are very unstable, I hear." And so he chattered on about war and rumors of war. Hannah listened with interest. He really was a very nice and interesting man. She heartily wished she could fall helplessly in love with him. Everything would be so easy then.

When lunch was over, Charles took his leave of the two women, looking gratefully at Hannah as she held Simba's collar while she shook his hand. Mrs. Butler looked grim and the instant that Charles had ridden behind the trees at the end of the lawn, she turned on her daughter.

"How dare you speak to me that way, young lady! Who do you think you are? I simply will not allow myself to be treated so rudely by my own daughter. And to think that Charles Montague asks you to sit with him in Garth Whitehead's box at the Kikuru Cup Races and you actually tell him that you have to go and fuss over horses! Horses!" Mrs. Butler was spluttering and turning purple.

"It is 1914, Mother. The twentieth century. There is more to life than just catching a man. We women will have the right to vote someday soon, and we can support ourselves and earn our own livings. We don't have to depend on a man for everything anymore. You should be proud of me. Daddy would be if he were here."

"Your father did you more harm than good with all those modern, newfangled ideas of his. He was just disappointed because you weren't a boy, that's all, and he tried to pretend you were. And I never had a chance with you, the way your father spoiled you."

This line of conversation always made Hannah furious, and her mother knew it. That's why she said it. "Daddy did not wish I was a boy. He told me so!" Hannah retorted, her fair skin turning pink with repressed rage as she watched her mother nod knowingly.

"Of course, dear, if he said so," her mother said sweetly, "but now it is time you behaved in a more ladylike manner. You will tell Garth Whitehead that you are otherwise engaged on the day of the races. His horses will be just fine. If they aren't, it will be too late to do anything about it anyway."

Hannah was suddenly tired. No matter what started it, they always ended up in the same old arguments. Her fury had abated now, and she just wanted to go back to work. She couldn't really believe she had actually accepted Charles's invitation anyway, and the price she was paying to have done so was already getting too high.

"I have to go to work now, Mother. I promised Jack Osbourne that I would come and look at one of his cows. He is afraid it has foot-and-mouth disease. Come on, Simba." Hannah pulled her hat out of her pocket and crammed it over her hair, which had frizzed up like cotton candy after the storm. She went around to the back of the house where the stable was. The syce had Kindye already saddled, and Hannah set off over the field behind the stable, taking the shortcut to the Osbourne farm.

It felt very nice to be out in the open air. She rode past the compound where the African people who worked on the Osbourne place had their huts, neatly enclosed by a stick fence. Through the fence she could see Rosie, her old ayah, sitting outside her son's hut. She waved, but Rosie was old and quite blind now, so she didn't see Hannah. Several little totos did, though, and came running over the field toward her. She waved them away, shouting, "*Mimi nakwenda* Bwana Osbourne. I'm going to Osbourne's!" They stopped and watched her ride away. Perhaps she would stop in and visit Rosie on the way back if it wasn't late. She could always tell Rosie everything. And she still was angry with her mother, so it would be nice to tell someone about it. *After all,* Hannah thought, *I would actually like to be married the way Mother wants, but I just feel so. . .so trapped.* She just couldn't suddenly metamorphose, like a butterfly, into one of those feminine women with the swishing silk skirts and soft feathery hats. And if she did, she could no longer work as a vet. How could she suddenly give it all up? Even if she did try, it was too late to change. *In fact,* she thought, *it has been too late to change all my life.*

The laughing face of Garth Whitehead flashed into her mind and before she thought about what she was doing, she suddenly wished she could change. It was a breath-catching, heart-stopping moment of wishing, and Hannah quickly shook it off. But it left her shaken.

❧

Rosie had been with the Butlers since Hannah was born and had looked after her until she had gone to England for her veterinary training. She lived with her son's family, now out in the village behind the Butler place, but Hannah still visited her often.

Hannah could see Rosie still sitting on a stool outside her round thatch hut watching a gaggle of totos playing with the rim of an old bicycle wheel. They were pushing it with a stick to see how long they could keep it rolling upright. The totos noticed Hannah when she interrupted a couple of hens scratching in the dirt, who cackled and flapped off indignantly, waking a couple of shenzi dogs lying in the shade. The dogs reluctantly barked and growled. The totos buzzed around her like a cloud of flies.

"Memsahib, memsahib, *tikki, tikki.*" They always begged her for the little coins that could buy the smallest piece of sugar cane or licorice, and she only encouraged them by handing out some every time she came. Rosie was smiling as she walked slowly and stiffly out to meet Hannah. They walked out toward a pair of thorn trees where they could see a bit of shade.

"What's the matter, missie?" Rosie asked, looking at Hannah slumped dejectedly against the dry, rough trunk of the tree.

"Oh, nothing really, I'm just hot, I suppose." Hannah sighed. Rosie knew better. She waited.

"Bwana Whitehead's black mare delivered a filly this morning. It had mucous in the air passage so he called me in to clear it. Poor little thing; I was almost too late." Hannah paused; Rosie waited. It was a comfortable silence. Hannah sometimes thought she loved Rosie more for her silences than anything she said. Hannah took her time to try to think through what she needed to tell Rosie, but then remembered that telling Rosie was almost the same thing as thinking it through for herself.

"Bwana Whitehead," she hesitated. "Garth," she whispered, trying out his name out loud. She could tell Rosie was watching her closely. She wished she didn't have such fair skin. She could feel a warm flush of emotion rising up her throat. "Garth likes to tease me about being a woman. And a vet. Usually, I hate being teased. I still do, but, well, I felt differently all of a sudden." Suddenly, Hannah's thoughts that had started as a few free-falling raindrops gathered themselves into a flash flood, pouring out of control down a dry, empty streambed.

"I often help him with his horses, you know, Rosie. He grew up in London and he really doesn't know a thing about animals, or even farming, especially in Africa. I know he wouldn't be able to manage without me. Perhaps that's the reason he teases me; he feels a little embarrassed needing me the way he does. What do you think, Rosie?"

Rosie opened her mouth to reply, but Hannah's flood was rushing too fast to be diverted. "Anyway, Rosie, today, when I was standing there next to him watching the little horse struggling to live, I felt suddenly that we really did perhaps have a bit of a bond, only I knew he was going to tease me the way he always does, so I rushed away as soon as I could.

I wish I were different, Rosie. I wish I weren't so shy and I could just tease him right back. But I get so tongue-tied. And then I turn a ghastly shade of red, and my hair is so uncontrollable I'm sure a decent hat would never stay on my head. So I always run away as quickly as I can."

Hannah paused for a moment. "But today as I left I really, really wished that I were different. And I honestly think that maybe he likes me. Maybe not the way he would one of the ladies at the Kikuru Country Club that Mother wants me to be like. But perhaps in a certain kind of way. After all, Rosie, you know he really couldn't handle those horses properly without my help."

Hannah stopped suddenly. Floods in Africa disappear as quickly as they come. But there was one more thing. "And now I have accepted an invitation to watch the races with Charles Montague from Garth's box. I wish Charles Montague were a little more like Garth—he is very nice, nice and dull." Hannah sighed discontentedly.

Rosie sat silently, waiting to be sure Hannah had really finished. Hannah watched her worn, wrinkled, kindly face anxiously. The the years had carved out the hollows in her cheeks, but her lips were still as full and wide as they must have been when she was twenty. And her eyes, though deep and dark, glittered and twinkled with as much intelligence and life as they ever had. Hannah watched her eyes, knowing from her lifetime of experience that she would only get the faintest hint from them of what was going on in that ancient mind. Hannah was a little nervous when she saw them softening and then even pitying her.

"What, Rosie? What are you thinking?" she blurted, suddenly impatient.

"You are right, missie, he couldn't do without your help. My cousin's son is a houseboy at Bwana Whitehead's, and he knows how things go over there. I hear things from his mother about Bwana Whitehead. He doesn't know much about animals, and he doesn't know much about this country."

"Yes, Rosie, that is true." Hannah was impatient for Rosie to get to the point, and her attitude was evident in her tone of voice. Instantly she stopped herself. "I'm sorry to sound so rude. I really don't know what has come over me today, Rosie." She caught a glimpse of pity in Rosie's eyes again, but she waited. Impatiently.

"My cousin," Rosie continued thoughtfully, "does not have a very high opinion of Bwana Whitehead. She says he drinks too much and gets angry, then he doesn't always pay her son his wages on payday. She says her son doesn't like working there."

"Well, Rosie, lots of people drink a little too much now and then. I've never known Bwana Whitehead not to pay me my fees. Is your cousin's son a reliable worker? Perhaps Bwana Whitehead is not entirely satisfied with him."

Rosie's eyes flashed an angry response to Hannah, but she said, "Missie, I think my cousin's boy is a hard worker. But if I were you, I would be very careful about becoming friends with Bwana Whitehead. My cousin tells me things about him. He is not a good man, missie."

Hannah felt frustrated. It was a silly idea to come and talk to Rosie about something she obviously knew nothing about. How could she? She was an African. What on earth could she be expected to know about the European culture? "I have to go now, Rosie," she said, going over and fetching Kindye from where she was grazing on a nearby patch of green grass. "Thanks for your advice. I'll keep it in mind." Passing through the little clutches of totos and chickens and a dog or two, Hannah whistled to Simba, who was lying in the shade with the other dogs.

As she rode down the dusty cart track in the late afternoon sunshine, Hannah thought about Garth. Now that she had actually spoken about him out loud to another human being, even if it was only to Rosie who didn't really understand, she found that her thoughts were bolder and more insistent. She couldn't just squeeze down the feelings of longing and hope that he had roused in her as she left his farm this morning. He needed help. He needed her help in particular. And if she could help him, who knows what that would do for him. After all, he might realize that those fancy ladies who spent their nights dancing and gossiping at the Kikuru Country Club were not what he wanted after all. Perhaps he would finally see that what he really wanted was a woman like her. A woman who knew Africa and how to live and thrive here. Perhaps he would realize that he needed her.

The hot, dusty field was no longer there for Hannah. In her mind's eye she and Garth were out riding up in the hills she could see through the haze on the horizon. Garth had settled down, and he now spent all his time with her. A good woman was all he needed, everyone would say. Who would have thought that Hannah Butler, the vet, would be the one to rescue him? Hannah Butler, I mean Hannah Whitehead, of all people, they would say. Well, I always thought there was more to her than met the eye, someone would point out. Hannah smiled, lost and happy in her daydreams.

But when she reached home the dreams vanished like the rain in the desert and she fell back into her old thoughts, and nothing good seemed possible anymore. She was just the vet—plain, but useful. Nothing more.

two

Hannah woke the next morning with Garth Whitehead on her mind. She remembered her silly daydreams from the day before and blushed to herself. But she could, perhaps even should, go over to his place and check on the little filly. It would be a nice gesture. Her heart fluttered a little at the thought of looking up into his face again so soon. Would he be able to tell what she had been daydreaming about? Of course not. She really was going balmy. The bright morning sun was already pouring in through the curtains, making everything look ordinary and matter-of-fact. All her fantasies withered and slunk away in the clear, sensible first light of day.

Hannah quickly threw off her covers and pulled the mosquito netting surrounding her bed out of her way. She had work to do. She had worked hard to become a vet, and she wasn't going to throw it all away now. She'd go out to the clinic and see who was there first, then in the hard glare of the midmorning she'd decide whether or not to go over to Garth's.

After breakfast, Hannah and Simba walked down to the clinic. Her father had finished building it just before he died, so it was quite modern and well equipped, especially considering this was East Africa. Hannah noticed the usual assortment of goats and a couple of cows, all with Africans holding onto them by ropes. But as she got closer she saw that they were all gathered around someone who was standing near the door. He was a tall, clean-cut man dressed in the white settler's uniform of a white shirt and khaki shorts. He and the Africans surrounding him were all looking down at an animal that must have quite an unusual problem, judging by the amount of interest they were showing it. "*Jambo! Nini shauri?* What's the fuss about?" Hannah called.

The Africans moved aside and the tall man walked toward Hannah. She tried to remember where she had seen him before, but she couldn't place him. She thought she knew everyone around here, so he must be new.

"*Jambo,* Miss Butler," he held out his hand and smiled timidly at Hannah. She shook his hand.

"I'm sorry; have we met before?" she answered.

"Oh, please forgive me for not introducing myself." The man flushed, turning nearly the color of his red hair. "I'm Dan Williams. I am the teacher at the mission school over by Limaru." Hannah smiled and thought how different he was from Garth. Garth would never look so flustered and awkward at the mere prospect of introducing himself.

"What is it I can do for you this morning, Mr. Williams? Or should I call you Reverend Williams?" Hannah found herself replying to him confidently and professionally, the way she would have liked to be able to speak to Garth.

"Oh, my, no!" He blushed and looked down at his dusty boots. "I'm just a teacher. It's that one of my students, you see. . ." He stopped and looked around.

"Mr. Williams!" Hannah spoke quickly, suddenly embarrassed for him. "I'm a vet. Not a doctor. I don't treat students."

"Oh, my goodness, how silly of me. It's not the student I want you to look at; I didn't mean that at all. It's that the student brought me an animal, an elephant, actually. It's the elephant, Miss Butler." At this point a little toto appeared beside Mr. Williams, pulling on a rope. Then a snaky gray trunk suddenly curled around Mr. Williams's knee. He bent down and brushed it away awkwardly and let the little calf elephant come between him and the toto.

Hannah knelt down on the ground and put out her hand. "My goodness, isn't she lovely!" she breathed. "She must only be a few weeks old. Where did you find her?"

The elephant put its trunk out and touched Hannah's hand. Her little gray ears flapped nervously out on the sides of her head, like the wings of an enormous bird. But her small, clear eyes peered curiously out from the wrinkly folds of the skin on her little face. Hannah caressed her trunk carefully with her fingers. *It's so alive and soft, just like a real baby,* she thought.

Dan Williams was kneeling down beside the little elephant now, his arm draped protectively over its back. He was smiling, and Hannah was touched by how gently he whispered into the creature's ear.

"Sophie, this is Miss Butler." Hannah noticed that his awkwardness had vanished as he spoke with the elephant. He turned to look at Hannah and said shyly, "I call her Sophie, because she looks so wise and so old, and Sophie means wisdom."

"That suits her," Hannah said, smiling at the little creature that was now reaching forward with her trunk to touch Hannah's face. "Where did you get her?"

"Pindanny," he nodded at the toto on the other side of Sophie who looked to be about ten or eleven years old. "Pindanny is one of the students in my school. He found her crying beside the body of her mother, who had been shot by a farmer. The farmer was apparently trying to frighten off a herd of elephants that was raiding his mealies. He didn't realize that he had actually hit one of them until he came back a few hours later to check the damage to his crop. He had Pindanny here with him and when he raised his rifle to shoot the baby, Pindanny rushed over and begged him to give him the baby." Dan smiled over at Pindanny. "You always were too softhearted, weren't you?"

"Anyway, Pindanny had no way of keeping Sophie, so he brought her to school and asked me if I would like her. I didn't have the heart to send her back to the bush to be supper for some local lions, so here she is."

"Well, I've never had an elephant for a patient before. What is it you need me to do for her?"

Dan Williams stood up and Hannah noticed his shyness return as he did. "I'm not terribly sure," he spoke uncertainly. "Well, in the couple of days since Pindanny brought her to me, well, she seems to be losing weight. I don't really know anything about baby elephants, and well, I don't know if I am feeding her the right things, really. I heard you were the nearest vet, even though you are a bit of a distance, and I wondered if you're not too busy if you could give me a bit of a hand with her." Hannah got to her feet, but Dan wasn't finished yet.

"This is a bit awkward, I'm afraid, but I don't have much of a salary and I couldn't really afford to pay you for your time, at least not what you probably ask for a fee." He stopped speaking and looked down at his boots. Hannah felt embarrassed for him. What an awkward fellow he was. No wonder he was a missionary. He probably didn't feel comfortable with ordinary society. Well, she supposed, they did have that in common. Suddenly she felt generous.

"That's all right, I don't mind helping you out with Sophie. In fact, I'm sure it will be my pleasure to get to know her too."

Dan smiled with relief. "Oh, thank you very much, Miss Butler! I am terribly grateful."

"There's just one thing, though. I've got rather a busy

morning ahead of me by the looks of all these people. Perhaps you wouldn't mind waiting for me to get to them first. Then I could take a few minutes to look at Sophie without rushing so much."

"Oh, of course, by all means!" Dan said quickly, pulling Sophie off to one side. "Is there somewhere I could wait for you?" Hannah showed him to a small shaded porch on the side of the building and called for some water for Sophie.

੩੦

It was almost noon by the time Hannah had finished in the clinic. She felt bad that she had kept Dan Williams waiting for so long. At about eleven o'clock she had impulsively sent out word to him to invite him to lunch. She shuddered at the thought of what her mother would say to her inviting a poor missionary over, but she couldn't keep him waiting so long without offering him a meal.

So at lunchtime she and Dan walked up the road to the house with Sophie and Simba trailing along behind them. Simba was not at all sure about this elephant that her mistress had so inexplicably befriended. It smelled too much like a wild animal for her to be sure about it, and she kept her distance. Sophie, on the other hand, behaved just like a naughty toddler, frolicking along, trying to tease the sedate old dog into playing with her and paying no attention to the warning growls that Simba emitted whenever Sophie got too close.

Dan had lost none of his awkwardness, and Hannah found it quite a novelty to be the one to be trying to put someone else at ease. She commented on Sophie's playful attempts to attract Simba's attention.

"I do hope I'm not inconveniencing you by imposing on you for lunch, Miss Butler," he worried.

"Not at all," Hannah replied, "I would not have invited

you if it was inconvenient. Besides, I sent word to Mother to expect you."

Dan looked dismayed. "Oh, my, I didn't realize I would be imposing on your mother as well! Perhaps I should just be on my way. I wouldn't want to be any trouble; after all, you are so kind as to give me some advice about Sophie. That's more than—"

"Mr. Williams!" Hannah interrupted him. He reminded her of the antelope she would catch grazing in the fields early in the morning. They would look at her in fear, torn between flight and food. "Mr. Williams, my mother loves to have guests. She often complains about how lonely she is, especially since my father passed away." She stopped. Now it was her turn to be embarrassed. Why was it that she still felt it necessary to bring her father into conversations?

"Oh, I'm awfully sorry to hear that," Dan was saying. "I can see I am intruding on you and your mother at a difficult time. I really won't stay. I'm terribly sorry I have been so terribly rude." His face was beet red, and Hannah felt a sudden surge of sympathy for him. "In fact, I'm sure Sophie will come around just fine. Please accept my condolences." Already he had turned and was reaching out to steer Sophie back in the direction they had come.

Now Hannah felt stupid. She put her hand on Dan's arm, "Mr. Williams, we have a misunderstanding. My father died five years ago. It was silly of me to mention it. I'm just used to speaking to people who know us. Please stay for lunch. I want you to. Besides, I would worry about Sophie if you just left with her like this."

Dan stopped and looked down at Hannah. For an instant the shyness in his eyes gave way to comprehension. They understood each other. Dan nodded. And then the shyness returned. They walked on together. The Butler house was in view, its red roof twinkling in the sunshine. But Hannah could already see the midday rain shower boiling up in the sky beyond.

"Look," she said, pointing the clouds out to Dan, "we'd better be quick."

They walked on more quickly, but Sophie was enjoying all the new sights and smells. She kept stopping and making little charges into the grass alongside the road. At one point she startled a flock of guinea fowl and gave herself as much of a fright as she gave them. Dan and Hannah laughed. She reminded Hannah of a huge kitten.

As they were watching Sophie, the wind roared through the treetops and swept down onto them. Within seconds huge drops of rain hurled themselves into the dry red dust of the road and then the heavens opened. Dan and Hannah were already running; even Sophie was running.

"Oh, Miss Butler, I'm awfully sorry," Dan was shouting through the curtain of rain, as if he had accidentally ripped the clouds open himself. He was pulling off his jacket and Hannah suddenly felt herself sheltered underneath it as they scurried along. She could feel Dan's breathing beside her as they ran, and she looked up just in time to catch the look of shock on her mother's face as she stood on the veranda watching them. They must be a sight, she realized, running in the rain, two people under one coat with a baby elephant charging along behind them.

They stormed up the steps, laughing gleefully. They stopped short. The laughter drained out of their faces as Mrs. Butler stood before them. Hannah realized what fun she had had, if only for a second. She didn't think she even remembered how to laugh.

But Sophie was carefully coming up the steps and Dan was looking startled and fearful. Hannah called out to Juma to bring a bowl of milk. Then she introduced Dan to her mother.

"I—I—I'm terribly sorry to be such an imposition, M—M—M—Mrs. Butler," stammered Dan.

"Oh, nonsense," Mrs. Butler brushed him off. "One more person isn't such a difficulty." She was looking him up and down as if he were a scrawny chicken being sold to her by the butcher. "I hear you are that missionary schoolteacher out by Limaru. They don't pay you much for being a missionary, do they? But then what have you got to spend your money on anyway, out in the bush where you live? Besides, you missionaries aren't allowed to do much besides teach the blacks anyway. Sit down. I wouldn't want it to be said that I didn't feed a man of the cloth when he came begging, would I?"

Dan took his seat, looking horrified. *Poor man,* thought Hannah.

"Mother! Let Mr. Williams at least wash up before he eats. He's soaking wet too."

She took Dan inside. They could have been in an English country gentleman's home, if they didn't look out the windows. Mrs. Butler let absolutely nothing into the house that could possibly be said to be African. There were the English oak table and Queen Anne chairs, not to mention the bone china, handpainted, set out on the oak sideboard. And then a lovely old grand piano took up fully a half of the drawing room. The wooden floors had intricately woven Persian rugs placed between the pieces of furniture, and Dan carefully stepped around them so he wouldn't get mud on anything.

Hannah showed him into a room with lacy curtains and a china washbasin steaming with hot water. It was set on a small table with a lace tablecloth and a white towel beside it.

"Here you are," she said, "I'll just wash up in the kitchen."

We always eat on the veranda. You know your way." Before Dan could apologize again, she was gone.

When Hannah came out of the kitchen, she could hear her mother talking excitedly outside on the veranda. *Good,* she thought, *she's at least trying to make Mr. Williams feel welcome.* But suddenly she caught the sound of a deep, familiar laugh and her heart missed a beat. Garth!

She hurried through the drawing room and outside. Dan was sitting at the table looking as though he was trying to squeeze himself into the most insignificant place he could find. Mrs. Butler was standing on the top step of the veranda, where the dripping of the rain off the roof was just about over, and in front of her was Garth, still mounted on his horse. They were both laughing at something on the front lawn, and when Hannah looked out, there was Sophie. Sophie had found a small puddle and was pulling water up from it into her trunk and trying to spray herself. Hannah laughed and rushed right past Dan to stand next to her mother.

"Han, old chap!" called Garth when he saw her. Hannah blushed and her mother looked at her with shock, as if Hannah had particularly asked Garth to refer to her as "old chap."

"I just popped over to thank you for coming to save my little filly yesterday," Garth went on, oblivious to the women's discomfort. "As I was saying to your mother, there is nothing like having a vet with a woman's touch, especially when it comes to delivering babies!

"I see you have another type of baby on your hands today!" Garth nodded at Sophie.

"Yes, isn't she sweet," said Hannah quickly, anxious to change the subject and use Sophie to make a good impression on Garth. "Mr. Williams, the missionary teacher at Limaru, brought her here this morning to see if I could help him decide on the best diet for her." She spoke about Dan as if he weren't there, justifying it by thinking that he was just too shy to be drawn into the conversation anyway.

Garth glanced at Dan, and Mrs. Butler quickly stepped back to show him the table. "Mr. Whitehead, please stay for lunch with us. We have plenty, as we were already expecting Mr. Williams. It would be such a pleasure for us poor women to have a man such as yourself for company. We really don't have much opportunity to entertain gentlemen." Hannah wanted to sink through the flagstone floor of the veranda at her mother's shameless speech, but she looked anxiously up at Garth, begging him with her eyes.

Garth smiled benevolently, enjoying the flattery, but he shook his head. "Thank you anyway, Mrs. Butler, but I have a lot to do, so I must pass up a visit today. As you must have heard, I have two horses entered in the Kikuru Cup Stakes next week and I have my work cut out just to get them ready." He nodded at Hannah. "I'll be expecting you to be there, of course, to make sure they are both in tiptop condition to run." Hannah blushed with pleasure at his attention, and Garth tipped his hat to her and spurred his horse.

Mrs. Butler and Hannah turned back to the lunch table. Mrs. Butler sat down angrily. Without even a glance at Dan, she launched into a tirade.

"There you are, Hannah Butler! What did I tell you! If you had the decency to even wear a simple dress, perhaps Mr. Whitehead might—just might—mind you, consider staying to have lunch with us. But what do you expect a man to do when a woman doesn't even bother to dress properly? And did you hear what he called you! I don't believe I have ever been so humiliated in my entire life! Old chap! Old *chap!*" Hannah cringed as Mrs. Butler's voice rose to a piercing squeal.

Looking furtively at Dan from under her lashes, Hannah

was startled to see a look of sympathy and warmth from him in return. She looked back at her mother. Mrs. Butler was drawing a deep, shaky breath to illustrate just how upsetting this whole thing had been for her.

"Mother!" hissed Hannah, "please, we have a guest." Mrs. Butler glanced over at Dan as if she only just noticed him.

"Yes, well, of course," she said, collecting herself again. "But really, Hannah, you do try me so."

There was silence for a few moments while Juma brought in the lunch dishes. Hannah lifted up her fork.

"Mr. Williams, would you be so kind as to give thanks for the meal?" Mrs. Butler said, and Hannah quickly put down her fork. They never said grace. What was her mother doing now?

"Father in heaven," began Dan, his head bowed, "thank You for this delicious food that You have blessed us with today. And thank You for the hospitality of Mrs. Butler and Miss Butler. Also, Lord God, I thank You for the generosity of Miss Butler. I pray You would give her guidance and wisdom and bless her in all her future endeavors. We pray to You in the name of Jesus Christ. Amen." He looked up and picked up his fork.

Hannah stared at him. She had never heard anyone speak to God in the familiar "You," as though He were actually living in the modern world with them. And to pray about such an earthy thing as an animal. She loved animals, too. After all, she was a vet. But to pray about them. At a meal. She picked up her fork again. Dan noticed her looking at him and glanced shyly at her. She looked away. *Funny,* she thought, *he didn't seem so shy when he prayed*.

Mrs. Butler was speaking. "Mr. Williams, surely it is your Christian belief that a woman should not wear men's clothing. I would appreciate hearing your opinion on that subject."

Dan stared at her. His face turned painfully red, and Hannah stopped feeling embarrassed about her mother and began to feel angry instead, but Dan managed to compose himself.

"Mrs. Butler, I don't like to judge other people by their appearance. But when a person becomes a Christian, I believe that the Lord makes them into a new creation. At that time He will make it clear to them if they are dressing inappropriately. Of course, modesty is always a virtue, whether one is a Christian or not." He fell silent.

"Hmph," said Mrs. Butler.

Hannah was curious. She had been to church, of course, although it had been a few years since she had attended regularly, she had to admit. But the old church that the Butlers sporadically attended didn't talk about God in nearly the same way Dan Williams did. At church God was spoken to only in the most old-fashioned language, Thees and Thous, and Hannah had never gotten even the slightest impression that God had any interest in speaking directly to people today. Especially not about things like someone's clothing, or animals. He merely disapproved if you did not do what you were supposed to do.

Mrs. Butler realized that Dan Williams was not going to be of much use as an ally against her daughter, so she reverted to ignoring him. Turning to Hannah, she resumed her usual topic of conversation. "Looks do make a world of difference to men, you know." She glanced at Dan. "Well, of course, not to a man like you, Mr. Williams, but then Hannah couldn't marry a missionary, and one as poor as a church mouse, no doubt."

Hannah knew that once her mother got going on this topic there was very little that could stop her. It was mortifying that she should carry on like this in front of Dan Williams, but luckily he was nobody important. Hannah had devised the best way to get through mealtimes many long years ago. She put her head down and ate as quickly as she could.

"Mrs. Worthington-Smyth called this morning," Mrs. Butler began. "You remember Mrs. Worthington-Smyth, don't you, Hannah? She is down from Nairobi visiting her daughter, Fiona, Jim Brown's wife. All she could do was complain about her son-in-law. She says he spends too much money on horses and gambling and poor Fiona has barely a dress to her name. He chums around with Garth Whitehead, you know, and those Whiteheads have money to burn, but Jim Brown is just not part of that social class and he shouldn't be pretending he is." Mrs. Butler passed Hannah a plate of roast beef and then handed her the gravy boat, all the while talking nonstop, not expecting a reply.

"Nevertheless, Harriet, I tell her, at least your daughter is married and associating with the proper class of people. You should be thankful for small mercies. I am the one who has more to worry about with Hannah. She doesn't even wear a dress. And a vet, mind you. I have to put up with far more than you do, Harriet, I tell her; I doubt Hannah will ever marry." She paused and took a deep breath. Hannah braced for the attack.

"Hannah, it is a disgrace the way you shame me so in front of my friends with your outlandish ways. Why can't you give up this veterinary nonsense and behave like a proper woman? You are twenty-five years old and it is time to grow up.

"I would just like to know how much longer you expect me to put up with this? I am the laughingstock of our circle. I can hear them whispering behind my back that I can't even bring up my daughter properly. Of course, I blame your dear father for much of it. He gave in to you far too much and there wasn't a thing I could do to stop him. But it's been five years since he passed on, and it's high time you put all his nonsense behind you and listened to me."

Hannah watched her pause for breath. Once or twice when she had been in her teens and still thought it was possible to change people, she had attempted to argue with her mother. But it hadn't even made the smallest dent in the convictions etched in the stony tablet of Mrs. Butler's heart.

Today there was Sophie to think on. She had no idea at what age young elephants were weaned from their mother's milk. She suspected they were quite old when they were. That would mean that the milk of the elephant would have to be extremely nutritious to keep such a creature healthy. Probably Dan had been feeding her cow's milk. She had lots of energy, but you could tell that she was quite thin.

Mrs. Butler was still talking when Hannah looked up from her empty plate. Mr. Williams was still eating, but since he had had no opportunity to talk with his meal, he too was almost finished. Mrs. Butler had hardly touched hers.

"Mother, I must get back to work, and Mr. Williams has a long trip ahead of him." Hannah glanced over and saw Dan rushing to eat his last few bites of mashed potato. "We still have to talk about Sophie's diet, too, so if you will excuse us, we must be off."

She stood up just as Dan popped the last mouthful in, and he hastily wiped his mouth and stood up too.

They walked back down the road to the clinic, talking about the various things Dan could try feeding Sophie. Sophie was walking along quietly beside them, tired from the long day she had had. Dan kept his hand on her head, stroking her ears now and then. Sophie moved her head around so he could scratch the parts she found itchy, and Hannah noticed how gently and thoughtfully Dan took her hints.

After Hannah had written down all the instructions and suggestions she had for Sophie's care, they stood in front of the clinic to say good-bye. Hannah knelt down and stroked Sophie on the trunk. Sophie reached up to touch Hannah's face.

"She's really taken to you," Dan was saying. "You have quite a way with animals. It is a gift."

Hannah stood up, blushing at the compliment. "Well, I am a vet, after all. Please send me a note to let me know how Sophie does with her new diet."

"I will," Dan replied, and they shook hands. "I am very grateful for your help, Miss Butler. Good-bye." He turned and left.

Hannah stood and watched the tall, awkward man and the small, gangly elephant calf disappear together into the haze of the afternoon. *It is a pity,* she thought, *that I can't be as relaxed and easy with Garth as I was with Dan Williams today.* She walked slowly back to the stables and whistled for Simba. She was going to head out on the calls she had this afternoon.

As she walked, she wondered. Maybe her mother was right. Perhaps she should try a little harder to look nice. What harm could there be in that? But an involuntary shudder shook her spine at the mere thought of trying to socialize with the women from the Kikuru Country Club. She pulled her hat down lower to shield her eyes from the unrelenting midday glare.

Then there was Rosie. She knew Rosie had other ways of helping a woman attract a man. She remembered what Rosie thought of Garth Whitehead. But perhaps, somehow, she could convince Rosie that she was mistaken about Garth and get her to give her a charm to get him to pay the right kind of attention to her. She knew a lot of the African women came to Rosie for help with a variety of problems, and she knew many times something actually worked for them.

There was definitely much that she couldn't explain about African medicine. Some people called it witchcraft, but Hannah didn't want anything quite that serious from Rosie. She just wanted one of those harmless little charms or potions that Rosie liked to do for her family when they needed a little extra help. And that was what she needed—a little extra help.

Ever since she had been a little girl, she had loved to sit outside the kitchen door where Rosie and the other Africans who worked for the Butlers would gather to eat and gossip. She would sit, leaning against the wall as quiet and unobtrusive as the little lizards that slipped in and out of the house every day. She always pricked up her ears and listened carefully when Rosie was giving someone advice about a problem with a cow or a husband or a sickness, or any of the little things that plague everyday life. The most intriguing thing to Hannah was the way the prescriptions often worked.

Of course Hannah had learned a more scientific worldview and rarely thought any more about Rosie and her old wives' tricks. But in the back of her mind she remembered that there were times when the African methods for healing illnesses did seem to work. Often this could be attributed to knowledge about the healing properties of a particular plant, or even to the patient's own desire to recover, but there were enough unexplainable cases to make Hannah wonder about how much she really learned about the scientific nature of the world.

She hadn't been a terribly faithful churchgoer ever in her life. She couldn't reconcile the power of prayer to her scientific worldview either. But then, she had never really known anyone personally who had been healed from anything through prayer, while she had seen Rosie's remedies work with her own eyes. Nevertheless, there were an awful lot of people in the world, Christian and African, who were claiming that there was more going on in this life than you could see with the naked eye. She thought of her friend, Fiona Brown, and now there was Dan Williams, too.

As she rode over the hot, dusty road to the farm where she had been heading, and looked over the grassy fields to the west, she could make out the cluster of trees and the white walls of the house in the center of them of the Whitehead Farm. What harm would there be in trying to get Rosie to get up one of her charms to make Garth fall in love with her? She had nothing to lose by doing that, did she? After all, if Fiona and Dan prayed to their God, how different was what Rosie did from praying, really? And as she made this decision to ask Rosie for her help, Hannah felt a strange sense of foreboding in her heart. In fact, she felt strangely ashamed of her decision, and the memory of Dan praying over Sophie at the lunch table slipped into her thoughts, but she quickly brushed it away. She was coming up to the farm now anyway. Already the dogs had noticed their arrival and were barking and running out to meet them. The hair on Simba's back stood straight up.

It certainly would be nice to have a little help, Hannah thought as she headed out to the barns behind the farmhouse. She remembered Dan's prayer for her. He spoke as though God were his personal friend, someone who actually took an active interest in his life. She wondered if God existed, and if He did exist, was He like Dan Williams said He was? Maybe one day she would have a chance to ask him about it. But here she was at the barn. Time to get to work.

three

Hannah drank the smell of the stables into her soul. The memory of her father was nearest to her in the earthy smell of horses, and she could almost see his familiar face through the steam rising from their sleek, shiny flanks in the cool morning sunshine. She and her Dad were out early, her little hand tightly held by her father's rough, wrinkled one, keeping her out of the way of the horses' swishing tails and deadly hooves. She never knew exactly where they were; the stables of all the farms they traveled to blended together into her memory. *If Father is in heaven,* she thought, *he would be caring for God's horses now, keeping them fit for racing over the high hills of heaven, hooves and manes flying ecstatically, glistening in the sunshine.*

When the minister spoke at her father's funeral of the mansion that was being prepared for those whom God would be taking to heaven, she thought of the stables with their labyrinth of rooms and the warm, comfortable welcome she always felt there.

A horse snorted and stamped its hooves impatiently and jerked Hannah into the present. It was the morning of the Kikuru Cup and the stables were already buzzing with activity. Stableboys led horses in and out of the stalls. Owners dressed in their Sunday best stalked through the halls, delicately avoiding steaming piles of dung. She saw the odd lady here and there, her filmy skirts carefully pulled just up to the ankles by small, white-gloved hands. Hannah noticed two of them making their way down to the far end of the stables where Garth's horses were being brushed by a couple of syces. She followed them. Despite the fact that she had taken special care with her appearance this morning, putting on her best trousers and a crisp white blouse rather than her usual khaki shirt and slacks, she felt uncouth and ugly behind these two ladies tripping so comically through the dirt and hay of the stable hall. She thought she recognized Leticia Charlesworth, one of Garth's lady friends whom she had seen once or twice at his place in the last couple of weeks. Sure enough, it was her. When they came to the Whitehead stalls, the women stopped.

"Yoo-hoo, Garth," Leticia called out, waving a lace hand-kerchief over her head. Garth stepped out from behind King, his black stallion, and waved at them. But just as he did, he caught sight of Hannah in the background.

"Han, old chap, there you are!" He left the horse and came striding up the hall, tipping his hat at the ladies as he brushed by them. "I've been waiting for you. Come, I'd like you to take a look at King's fetlock. I'm sure it's nothing to worry about, but nevertheless, I'd like your opinion."

He took Hannah by the elbow and tipped his hat again to the ladies as he steered her past them. Hannah floated along, attached to reality only by the feel of his hand touching her arm. As they bent down, side by side, to look at the small bump on the horse's leg, Hannah was barely able to keep her eyes focused as her mind took in the concern in Garth's voice and the way he looked at her face, trying to read her opinion as she made it up. She was vaguely aware of the two young ladies who were standing out by King's stable door whispering to each other as they never took their eyes off Garth. But for Hannah the whole scene was wrapped in the warm, welcoming scent of the morning stables, adding romance and familiarity to the warmth in her heart.

She and Garth rose together to stand next to the beautiful, shining black horse, and Garth looked into her eyes with his own filled with care and worry. Hannah knew then that she was in love with him. The two ladies still stood in the background, silent now, like lovely lifeless dolls, but Garth looked only at her. She was real and alive. She was the one who held the key to his happiness, his horses. She was the one he was interested in.

"I think it is just an insect bite, Garth," she said softly, using his name for the first time, watching the relief flood his face. "I'll put something on it, which may help the swelling a little, and I'm sure he'll be ready to run this afternoon."

"I was terrified he had injured it. I'm so relieved, I could kiss you!" And without missing a beat, he put his hands on Hannah's shoulders and bent down and kissed her lightly on the lips. Hannah stood still. The soft touch of his lips on hers created a rushing flood of emotion that raced through her body. She thought for a moment that it would knock her to the floor. She could still feel his lips on hers and his breath and his eyes and his hands.

He was laughing now. "Now, now, Han, you look as though you're about to slap my face for taking liberties. But really, you'll forgive me, won't you? I couldn't help myself. Come, let's get going and fix King's leg. Where's your bag?"

Still speechless, Hannah bent down and picked up her black bag. She rummaged around until she found what she needed. Meanwhile, Garth walked over to the two women and started to chat with them. Hannah could hear them laughing and talking above her as she worked on King, but it was all so far away now. When she was done, she stood up.

"There you are, King, you'll be fine." Hannah spoke aloud to catch Garth's attention. Immediately, he turned around.

"Han, old chap, you know Leticia Charlesworth, don't you?" Hannah nodded. So did Leticia. "And I'd like to introduce you to her cousin, just arrived from England. Felicity, this is Hannah Butler, my vet and right-hand woman." The two ladies tittered and Felicity mumbled something appropriate, but already Hannah was blushing with shame. She was such a bumbling fool in the company of women like this. How could she possibly think Garth saw anything but a useful vet in her?

"Well, we're off to the races!" announced Garth, stepping out of the stall and offering the two ladies his arms. "Cheerio, Han, thanks a million!" Then he paused and looked back over his shoulder. "Oh, I almost forgot; I'll be seeing you later! Montague told me you'd be joining us in the box! See you then, Han, old chap. Cheers!" And they were gone.

Hannah, the syce, and the jockey were left in the stall. One of his hired people was all she was to him. Hannah blushed with embarrassment at the thought of how she had felt only minutes ago. Quickly, she packed up her bag and slipped away down the hall and out into the fresh air, where she found Simba faithfully waiting for her at the door.

"Hannah, I've been looking for you!" Hannah looked up to find Fiona and Jim Brown coming towards her. She had known Fiona since they had been to school together, and she was grateful for Fiona's faithfulness in keeping up their friendship. She had been a bridesmaid at Fiona's wedding when she had married Jim Brown, a local farmer. Fiona's mother had been horrified by her daughter's choice of a husband, thinking he was socially far beneath her. But lately Jim had been trying to improve his social standing to suit his mother-in-law, and had been seen often in the company of Garth Whitehead at the Kikuru Country Club.

"The races are about to begin, Hannah!" Fiona said, taking

Hannah by the arm. "Charles told me you were coming to Garth's box with him. I hope Garth doesn't have you slaving away doing something for him! Jim says you've been practically running the stables for him these days."

"Oh, no, not really!" said Hannah, blushing far more furiously than the compliment warranted. She noticed Jim glance curiously at her, but in a moment they were swept along by the crowds surging around the track. Hannah excused herself, explaining that she had to change before she met Charles.

A little while later she made her way up to Garth's box at the top of the grandstand. He was ensconced up there, still in animated conversation with Leticia and Felicity. But Charles Montague, who had been anxiously watching for Hannah, had already seen her and was rushing over to greet her. Hannah forced herself to smile at him.

"Hannah, why, you look lovely this morning!" he beamed at her while he took in the rather old-fashioned navy blue dress she was wearing with the white sailor's collar and white buttons down the side of the straight skirt. It wasn't the height of fashion, but it was crisp and clean looking. Mrs. Butler had insisted that Hannah buy a small white hat to wear with it, as well as white shoes. Hannah suddenly felt shy being surveyed with such obvious satisfaction. For an instant she had the feeling she was a racehorse being looked over by a prospective buyer, but she shook the feeling away and smiled back at Charles. After all, if she was going to try to be a part of this crowd, it would not be her skill as a vet, nor would it be her intelligent conversation that would attract people. It would be the way she looked. She would just have to get used to being looked over like so much horseflesh and try to feel grateful when she was approved.

"Come along, my dear," said Charles, taking her by the

elbow and leading her fussily over to the chairs he had saved for the two of them. "The races are about to start and I'm so frightfully glad you've arrived in time. It is so exciting to be able to cheer on Garth's horses. I do hope they win." He leaned confidentially over her as he pulled out her chair for her and whispered, "I've placed a small wager on each of his horses to win. Of course knowing that you personally are his veterinarian, I feel my wager is quite safe!" He laughed gleefully at his very small joke and Hannah smiled vaguely. She was grateful to see that they were seated next to Fiona and Jim Brown. Quickly, she turned to greet them. But as she did, Garth suddenly noticed her arrival.

"There you two are!" he said, shaking Charles's hand and smiling approvingly at Hannah's dress before looking at her face. "And you brought Han with you! Good! Good!" He pulled out another chair and sat down next to Jim. Within seconds the two men were engaged in an intense conversation about the quality of the other horses in the race. Hannah wished she could strike up a few words with Fiona to avoid listening to Charles, but Fiona was concentrating on her husband's conversation.

Hannah was surprised to notice how unhappy Fiona looked. She was watching Jim with a kind of sullen resentment. Jim, on the other hand, turned to her now and then with a bright smile and asked her how she would like to make some good money today on the races.

"Cheer up, darling, Garth and I know what we're doing. We'll be coming out ahead of the game after today. We simply can't lose. Not today—not against this bush-league competition." Then he turned to Garth with another morsel of gossip he had picked up that morning from one of the syces he had been talking to. Fiona pursed her lips and glared at Garth angrily for a moment before he glanced her way. She quickly looked down at the track where the horses in the first race were being led to the gates. Beside Hannah, Charles was rummaging through his program, making exclamatory noises here and there and asking Hannah if she knew this or that horse.

"Are you feeling alright?" Hannah said impulsively to Fiona. Fiona looked up, surprised, as if she hadn't noticed Hannah's presence until now.

"Oh. Yes. Thank you," she responded automatically.

"Don't you like the races?" Hannah tried again. Why on earth was Fiona suddenly behaving so strangely?

"Yes. I mean, no. Jim does. Not me." She stopped. Then added. "I like horses. It's just the betting I don't like. It seems like a waste of money to me."

Jim caught the last few words and turned to Fiona. "Now, darling, don't start that again." There was an edge to his voice. Garth leaped to the rescue.

"Don't you be worrying your pretty little head about that, my dear. Jim and I have everything under control. And Hannah here is keeping the horses in tiptop condition, aren't you, Han, old chap?" His quick glance at Hannah brought the tidal wave rushing to her face in a flood of color. But no one noticed and he continued to address Fiona.

"You must realize, my dear, that farming in this infernal country is far more of a gamble than betting on the odd horse race. If you need a little bit of pin money here and there, there is no easier way to get some than a good old-fashioned horse race. Now, my dear, don't be giving your poor husband a hard time over it. He's only doing it for your sake, you know. And you must let a man have his fun now and then."

He turned away from Fiona and back to Jim with an air of having dealt with the problem in a professional way. Fiona was sullen. Hannah was suddenly swamped again by the waves flooding her thoughts with Garth's kiss.

"Hannah! There you are at last! I was afraid you might be late!" Hannah looked up, dismayed to see her mother leaning precariously over the railings that separated the box from the regular stands. "Goodness me, Mr. Whitehead, I didn't mean to interrupt. I just noticed my daughter. Hello, Jim, Fiona. I saw your poor mother the other day, Fiona. Mr. Whitehead, it is such a pleasure to see you again. I do hope you'll drop by again for a visit when you are able to stay longer." She turned to Fiona. "He's such a busy man, you know!"

"Have you heard the latest news from home? There are rumors of war against the kaiser. Oh dear, what shall we do if there is war? I am so frightfully worried. Aren't you worried, Mr. Whitehead? Will you go and fight?"

Garth glanced at Jim. Hannah thought she detected a look of mutual irritation pass between the two men, and she felt like sliding under her chair with embarrassment at her mother. But there was no escape now.

"I've been hearing those rumors for years, Mrs. Butler," Garth was saying. "I really don't think it will amount to much. We are far too civilized to stoop to shooting each other in this, the twentieth century. And if those Huns are barbaric enough to start a war, I'm sure we'll put them in their place in short order. We won't even know about the war here in Africa until it is all over. At least I certainly hope that is the case, because I have better things to do than risk my life in a ridiculous war in Europe." The grandstands were filling up rapidly now with the crowds.

"Harriet, dear, there you are. I'm so sorry we're late." Hannah looked up with relief to see Maureen Fitzhugh bustling between the rows of benches to reach her mother.

Garth and Jim stood up and nodded politely. Garth looked at Mrs. Butler. "It has been lovely chatting with you," he said, smiling at her insincerely. Hannah cringed at the tone of Garth's voice. It would be so much easier to fit in with Garth's crowd if her mother were less embarrassing. No wonder she was such a social failure. Mrs. Butler was making her way away from the box, and Hannah suddenly felt the overwhelming need to get away also. But there was no escape.

Instead, she shrank within herself while Charles put his arm possessively around her shoulders and began pointing out the various horses he knew who were starting to line up near the starting gates. Hannah only had eyes for the magnificent black King. He was prancing and tossing his head in anxious anticipation of his run, the energy in his sleek black body barely held in check by the tiny jockey perched precariously on his back.

All of a sudden the gates swung open, and King burst out onto the track. As if he were sailing with the wind, he slid into first place next to the railing. On her left, Garth, Leticia, and Felicity were shouting and cheering, enjoying themselves immensely. But Jim was as tense as a lion stalking its prey.

"Come on, King, keep it up. Run for me, King, you can win this one." He spoke quietly and intensely, as though he and King were the only two beings at the track. Beside him, Fiona sat silent and grim.

King sailed gracefully and easily over the finish line, and Hannah leaped up to join the cheering crowd. Leticia and Felicity were kissing congratulations on Garth's cheek, even as he shook hands with everybody within reach, including Hannah.

Glancing behind her for a moment, Hannah noticed that Jim slumped back into his chair, exhausted with relief, before rising to shake Garth's hand. Fiona just smiled, her face tight but relieved. For an instant they were a stark contrast to the happy crowd around them, but quickly they adjusted their expressions to fit in.

"Thanks for everything! I don't know where I would be without you, Han. I must run!" Garth bent over and kissed her cheek, and he was gone. They all sat back down to watch the presentation of the cup.

"Would you like to join me this evening for the victory party at the club, Hannah?" Hannah turned, startled for a moment. She had completely forgotten about Charles.

"Oh, yes, thank you. That would be lovely," she replied without thinking as she watched Garth wend his way down through the hands reaching out of the crowd to congratulate him. Instantly Hannah regretted her words, but she couldn't call them back.

Most of the evening she stood next to Charles, who escorted her chivalrously around the room making small talk with all the right people. But Hannah always had one eye on Garth, and in her heart of hearts it was Garth she was standing beside, even as she watched him chat and laugh with his guests. Leticia and Felicity were always one step away from him, ready to bask in his smile whenever he turned in their direction. Hannah watched and wished. It was a long, long evening.

Late that night Hannah was at last in her own bed alone with her thoughts and too tired to sleep. She lay and listened to the distant night noises of insects buzzing, faraway grunts and calls of the animals, and the myriad of birds that filled the night. The mosquito net over her bed rippled in the wind like a ghostly veil, and inside, her mind moved and danced between fantastic dreams and longings.

Garth was elusive, but never far from her mind. She remembered the way he made her feel as though she were the most important person in the world to him one minute, and the next he hardly realized that she existed. But there was one thing she did know for certain: If Garth Whitehead ever should decide that he wanted her, she would be his. She wouldn't even give it a second thought. She would be gone. But until then, if that day should ever come, she must keep her feelings to herself. Could she possibly do that? She dreamed of his surprise and joy to find that it was she that he really loved and that she had always loved him.

Far off in the distance a lion roared. She shuddered and was catapulted out of her dreams of Garth. Her thoughts moved to Jim and Fiona. Something was very wrong. She felt bad about Fiona. Fiona had always been a good friend to her, but she never really worked much at being a good friend in return. Perhaps she should try to change. Perhaps Fiona could use someone to talk to. She would go out and have tea with her in a couple of days. Of course Fiona was one of those people who was terribly involved in the church, and she likely had many friends. *But still,* Hannah thought, *she has been a good friend and if she is unhappy, it is only a kindness to go and visit her, even if she does have other church friends.*

And that brought her mind to Dan. She wondered how Sophie was doing on her new diet. She wished she could talk to Garth freely and easily the way she talked with Dan. But then, Dan wasn't Garth. At last she drifted to sleep.

four

The next few weeks Hannah only saw Garth occasionally. The horse racing season was over, and he didn't need her help as much anymore. He had done fairly well at the Kikuru Cup, but King's win was his only first-place finish. She heard rumors from Rosie that there were wild parties at his house, and once she had met him in town. He had Leticia with him. Hannah had been shopping for groceries in the little duka when the two of them had walked in, arm in arm.

"Han, old chap!" Garth had called to her as the storekeeper was tallying up her bill. "How are you? Lettie, you remember Han, don't you?"

"Yes, of course, we met at the horse races. Hello, Han," Leticia answered, smiling casually at her. Hannah knew from the way she used Garth's nickname for her that they were close friends.

Hannah tried to tell herself that it was inevitable that Garth would fall for someone like Leticia. After all, even as she had fallen in love with him she had known she had no hope of ever having her love returned. Still, it didn't make it any less painful. She braced herself for the day she would hear news of his engagement to Leticia.

❧

She had gone over to Fiona's one day after the races. Fiona greeted her kindly enough and invited her into the little farmhouse for tea. Hannah had always liked Fiona's little house. It was so unlike the way her mother kept their house. Fiona tried to be a part of Africa. There was no ceiling inside and the thatched roof was visible as well as the supporting beams in the roof. It was cool and comfortable, with more air circulating in the heat of the day. The furniture they sat upon was a mixture, with African hides strung over frames and lovely polished English end tables scattered here and there. The whitewashed walls were incongruously decorated with English prints and Jim's hunting trophies, and there was a large wildebeest skin rug on the floor. It was a newlywed's home: bachelor furniture mixed with elegant wedding presents.

Fiona served tea and little gingerbread biscuits on beautiful English china decorated with delicate pink roses.

"It is lovely to see you, Hannah," Fiona began politely. "I hope you've been well lately. I feel very remiss that I haven't been over to see you and your mother for so long. How is your mother?"

"She's very well, thank you," replied Hannah, wondering how to break through Fiona's polite chatter. It wasn't at all like the warm, genuine friendliness she was used to from Fiona. They chatted on for a few minutes about their respective mothers and their mothers' health. Hannah sipped her tea and nibbled on her biscuit. This was exactly the sort of conversation she detested. She decided she would have to be the one to initiate a more personal subject.

"F—Fiona," she began, stammering a little, "I am worried that you are not feeling quite well. I hope there is nothing wrong."

Fiona looked surprised and then smiled genuinely for the first time that afternoon. She reached out and took Hannah by the hand. "Thank you for inquiring, Hannah. You are a kind friend, but I really can't discuss my troubles with anyone, although I wish with all my heart I were free to do so. It would lift the burden so much just to be able to talk, but pray for me when you remember, Hannah. I would be grateful for that."

"I will," Hannah mumbled, blushing at the idea of praying. Since she had made an effort to come to this point with Fiona, she decided she must try one more time to help her.

"I hope there is nothing the matter between you and Jim. I know I am the last person who would be of any help to you if there was, but I would do anything within my power to help if you would only feel free to call on me."

The pained look on Fiona's face told Hannah she was right in her guess, but Fiona quickly hid it behind a falsely cheerful smile.

"Thank you so much for your concern, Hannah. It is a comfort to me to know you care about my troubles. I must only ask you to pray that I may have the strength to face everything." Fiona was clearly determined not to discuss her situation, so Hannah didn't press her any more about it. They spoke about the weather and the prices that farmers could be expected to receive for their crops this year. Fiona had lost her sparkle and enthusiasm for life, and Hannah could see that it was an effort for her just to keep the conversation going. As soon as she had finished her tea, Hannah stood up.

"Thank you for the tea, Fiona. I'd better be getting back to work."

"I thank you for coming to see me, Hannah," Fiona said as they walked together out onto the little veranda made by the overhanging thatch of the roof. "It means more than you know that you care about me enough to come and see me. I can only ask you to pray for me. And Jim also."

Hannah took her hat out of her back pocket and plastered it over her blond head. "I will, Fiona," she mumbled shyly— glad, yet embarrassed, that Fiona assumed that she prayed.

And she did, later that night as she pulled her mosquito net around her bed. "Lord, God, please help Fiona. Amen."

❧

"I don't care whether she has an animal in there or not! Let me through!" It was Mrs. Butler's voice. What on earth was she doing here at the clinic? Hannah braced herself, and the next instant Mrs. Butler burst into the room where Hannah was just bandaging up a large dog's leg.

"Hannah, have you heard the news! We're at war! Oh, dear, I just had to rush down and let you know. What is the world coming to! The news was sent over the wireless this morning. Everyone who is able to fight is asked to do his duty for the king and sign up. What a terrible, terrible day this is! War!"

Hannah opened her mouth to respond, but Mrs. Butler didn't wait.

"I am going into town to see if I can find out some news. I know the Fitzhughs have a son at home in Ireland. I must go and see Maureen. Oh, Hannah, this is the first time in my life that I am grateful you weren't a boy. Good-bye!" She rushed out the door. Hannah was left staring into the soft brown eyes of the large black Labrador on her table. She shook her head and stroked his, glad as always that she spent her days with animals, not people.

She wondered if Garth had heard the news yet. He had said he wouldn't be risking his life in a war, but perhaps now that war was a reality, he would change his mind. After all, one did have a duty to defend one's country, and Garth would surely want to join the cause. She wished she were the one who would be seeing him off to war. He would look so handsome in a uniform, and she would stand on the plat- form with all the other women, waving good-bye as the train pulled away from the station, tears streaming down her face, and Garth would dream of coming home to her.

Daydreams. Her whole life was daydreams now that she had fallen in love with Garth. She had to admit that they were incredibly unfulfilling. She lifted the dog gently down onto the floor, then reached into her pocket and gave him a biscuit. She led him limping, but wagging his tail gratefully, out to the waiting room, where his master was waiting for him.

*

On Sunday, Mrs. Butler, who had not heard much more news about the war in Europe, was nevertheless still in a terrible uproar about the whole situation. She decided to go to church to pray for the boys who would be off to fight. She insisted that Hannah go with her, and so Hannah found herself sitting uncomfortably in a pew in the second to last row of St. Bartholomew's Church, where she and her mother very occasionally attended. As the choir marched up the center aisle following the altar boy with the cross, Hannah made a quick inventory of the people in the pews in front of her. It wasn't easy to tell who everyone was from the back, and it was made a little more difficult by the fact that the church was as full as at Christmas and Easter services. Everyone must have had the same idea as her mother. She thought she recognized Jack Osbourne and his wife Mary, who had the farm next door to she and her mother. She also thought she saw Fiona Brown, but her husband, Jim, didn't appear to be with her. Mr. and Mrs. Fitzhugh slipped sheepishly into the pew next to Hannah and her mother. They were late and came in after the choir. Mrs. Butler nodded a greeting.

The church service proceeded like clockwork. Hannah followed the prayers in the prayer book and sang the hymns in the hymnal. Everything was beautiful, solemn, and ordered.

It made her wonder about Dan Williams. How did his informal prayers fit into this kind of a service? And whose prayers did God listen to? Did He find Dan's prayers too familiar? After all, He was, assuming He existed at all, the God of the entire universe, and a small, personal prayer from nobody in particular in the middle of Africa was probably beneath His dignity.

Hannah's thoughts wandered to Sophie. She wondered if she were doing well on her new diet. She really ought to send Dan a note asking about Sophie. She resolved to do so that very afternoon. Perhaps she would even invite Dan over for tea. After all, she had enjoyed his company, and an afternoon of not being alone with her mother, especially in the excitable condition she was in these days, was always a good thing.

When at last the choir filed out and the congregation followed, Hannah found herself walking outside into the heat of the day next to Fiona Brown. They greeted each other warmly and one after the other they shook Reverend Cosgrove's hand. Then they were standing together in the churchyard. "Warm weather, isn't it?" Fiona said politely.

"It certainly is," agreed Hannah. They stood in silence for a minute. A guilty thought slipped quickly into Hannah's mind. Before she let herself think it through, she spoke it aloud.

"I was just wondering how Mr. Whitehead is doing? Have you seen him lately?" Hannah felt shameless, but she knew if he were engaged, Fiona would mention it. A shadow crossed Fiona's face. Hannah held her breath.

"He's very well, I'm sure, although I can't say I've seen much of him recently," she responded with a chill in her voice. "Jim sees him much more than I do. If you'll excuse me, I really must be going." She smiled the same falsely cheerful smile that Hannah had seen when she had been to tea. "Good afternoon, Hannah." And quickly she turned and walked away.

Hannah stared after her, hurt and surprised, but a minute later a familiar voice rang out behind her.

"Miss Butler, Hannah, I've finally caught up with you!" Hannah's heart sank even lower as she steeled herself and turned to face Charles Montague.

"Good morning, Mr. Montague," she replied stiffly. She hadn't seen him since the day of the races. He had driven her home after the victory party at the club and asked if he could call on her again, but she mentioned that she was very busy at the moment. After that, he had sent word to her several times asking to call, but she had managed to avoid him, until now.

"Miss Butler, I have terrible news for you. I am going home to join up and defend my country against the dreaded Hun." He paused, waiting for Hannah to absorb the import of this tremendous announcement. When Hannah merely nodded, he tried to clarify his point.

"I am leaving at the earliest possible moment. There is a ship leaving Mombasa next week and I have secured a passage on it. Of course we will not see each other again until the war is over. I trust it will be over by Christmas. Nevertheless, I would be grateful if you would consent to correspond with me. I know that to receive letters from you whilst I am on the field will sustain me in my loneliness. Of course, with my family connections I don't expect to be one of the foot soldiers. But I would look forward to your letters, and of course, you will have mine in return."

Hannah fixed her smile rigidly. Fortunately, her mother had just finished speaking with the Fitzhughs when she spotted Hannah and Charles.

"Oh, Mr. Montague, how lovely to see you. Isn't this news of the war a dreadful shock? You are going home, of course, a man of your standing and family would be anxious to do his duty." Charles nodded and opened his mouth to reply, but Mrs. Butler took no notice. "I do hope you won't forget all about those of us here in Africa who will be praying for you and for the country. You will write to us," she nodded toward Hannah, "won't you, Mr. Montague? We will be so anxious to hear how you are." She stopped to take a breath. Charles seized the moment.

"Of course I am going, Mrs. Butler, and Hannah and I have agreed to correspond whilst I am away."

"Oh, Mr. Montague, we will look forward to your letters. We are very grateful that an important personage such as yourself should think of us, aren't we, Hannah, dear?" Hannah nodded dumbly and Charles took advantage of the lull to make his escape. Tipping his hat, he announced to Hannah that he would call on her to take his leave, and much to Hannah's relief he slipped away through the dispersing congregation.

Mrs. Butler and Hannah made their way out of the churchyard to their waiting buggy. Jolting home along the rutted road, Hannah slipped away into her daydreams again. It was becoming a serious habit with her these days, especially when she didn't want to think about other things, such as Charles Montague, for instance.

She drifted into a future where she and Garth were married, or at least engaged. He was grateful to her for rescuing him from his wild ways. Hannah pictured Felicity and Leticia watching wistfully as she and Garth swept by them on the street, arm in arm and so engrossed in each other that they hardly noticed who was around them. Garth would decline invitations from the crowd who partied every weekend at the country club because he and Hannah had better things to do. They had his horses to care for and meals to enjoy together and quiet evenings talking together. Hannah could just imagine the warm joy of his caresses, his kisses, and the things he would whisper in her ear about how much more wonderful it was to be with her than with anyone else. *Oh, the blissfulness of it all,* Hannah sighed to herself, *if only it could be true.* If only she could wish hard enough to make it happen.

The buggy came around the bend and the red tile roof of her home glinted in the morning sunshine. It was still another good hour before lunch would be served. Hannah couldn't face the thought of spending it with her mother, listening to the local gossip. There was only one person she would like to talk about, and there was little chance that her mother would have heard anything about him. Her friends didn't associate with anyone in his circle. She decided to pop over to visit Rosie before lunch. Perhaps Rosie's cousin would have passed on some news.

Rosie was sitting outside her hut as usual. The compound was as full as ever, with dogs and chickens and totos running in and out of the huts. Together she and Rosie walked out towards the shade of their thorn trees, chatting for a few minutes about Rosie's family. At last Hannah decided she must plunge in.

"How is your cousin getting on at Bwana Whitehead's these days?" She tried to make her voice sound casual, but Rosie wasn't fooled for a minute. Rosie turned to face Hannah.

"Memsahib, Bwana Whitehead is bad news. He is only interested in parties and spending money and women. You are not interested in him, are you?"

Hannah picked a twig sticking out of the tree behind her. She tried to explain her feelings in a positive light. "I spend quite a lot of time with him during the racing season, you know, Rosie. He loves horses and so do I. We spend time talking and planning for the races, and he really values my opinions. He listens to me and he needs my help. We have a friendship and I see a side of him that other people don't. He is kind and gentle and thoughtful. Other people only see the social, outgoing, partying side of him. But there is much more to him than just that. I know because I have seen it, Rosie." She paused, took a deep breath, and plunged on. "I remember the charms you give people when they need some help, Rosie. I want to try one."

Hannah looked anxiously into Rosie's deep, dark eyes. She could never fathom what was going on in her mind. She would just have to wait for her to tell her, and Rosie was never in much of a hurry. She lived in African time, not rushed, scheduled European time. Hannah sighed impatiently and waited.

At last Rosie took a deep breath. "It doesn't help you if you don't believe, memsahib."

"How can I believe if I don't have a chance to try it?"

There was a pause, and Rosie shook her head. But when she looked up at Hannah, she was smiling. "Alright, missie, you can try. Perhaps it will help you."

"Thank you for your help, Rosie," Hannah said, falling into step with her as they headed out into the sunshine toward the shamba. Rosie went inside the dark hut and returned with a small cowrie shell that she had strung on a leather thong. It was a beautiful shell of golden brown with black stripes along the edge where it curled outward.

Hannah took it and thanked Rosie as she tied it around her neck and tucked it inside her shirt. A heavy and unhappy feeling overcame Hannah as she left the shamba. She walked slowly, her head hanging down and her feet dragging in the dusty path. She suddenly felt very, very tired.

Because she wasn't paying any attention to where she was going, she was startled by the sudden trumpet of an elephant right in front of her. She nearly jumped out of her skin, and it took her a couple of startled seconds to see Sophie, the baby elephant, come running toward her along the path.

"Oh, my goodness, Sophie, what are you doing here? You frightened the daylights out of me!" Hannah bent down to scratch her behind her ears. Sophie moved her head from side to side like a cat being stroked. Hannah had to laugh at her. "Sophie, you silly little thing! You are an elephant, for crying out loud, not a kitten. You'll be purring for me any minute if you keep this behavior up." Sophie reached up and caressed Hannah's face with the end of her trunk.

Suddenly Hannah felt better. This was reality—warm, healthy, living reality. The little shell still felt a bit strange around her neck, but it had warmed to the temperature of her skin and it was easier to ignore. Perhaps she would throw it away. It was, after all, in comparison to the reality of life before her, a silly thing to believe in. Her life was looking after animals, not chasing after dreams that could never come true. Hannah stood up with a lighter heart. The red tile roof of the house was visible along the path up ahead, and Hannah and Sophie walked together under the shady trees. Hannah was glad to know that Dan would be on the veranda with her mother and she wouldn't have to face lunch alone with her.

Dan was indeed on the veranda, but Mrs. Butler was nowhere to be seen. Dan stood up when he saw Hannah and Sophie appear through the trees at the bottom of the garden.

"Good afternoon, Mr. Williams," said Hannah as she came striding up the lawn. "It is so nice to see you again. I see Sophie is looking well too!"

"Y—yes, sh—she is," stuttered Dan, turning red with the embarrassment of having to speak. "It is th—th—thanks to the new diet you gave her. It seems to agree with her. I really appreciate it, Miss Butler." His face was crimson by now and Hannah had to laugh to herself. Why did she feel so glad to see him? He was, after all, so inept and shy.

"We are just about to sit down to lunch. I hope Mother's invited you to stay." she said confidently.

"Oh, yes, she did, but I didn't mean to intrude. I went to the early service this morning so that I could get here and back with Sophie before dark. I really didn't intend to be here for lunch, but your mother was kind enough to invite me to stay. She said she had to go inside, though." Dan rushed headlong through this speech.

"Well, it was very nice of you to come and visit. I am so glad to be able to see Sophie for myself. It seems as though she hasn't forgotten me," Hannah replied.

"Oh, yes, but I did have another reason for coming to see you—at least, I think I do—but I find that it might be too much trouble for you now that I think about it."

Suddenly the door opened and Mrs. Butler swept out onto the veranda. "Oh, there you are, Hannah! What on earth were you doing? I had all the servants looking everywhere for you!" Mrs. Butler didn't bother with Hannah's reply before plunging onward. "As you see, Mr. Williams is here with that elephant of his again. I felt it only polite, considering we hadn't dined yet, to invite him to stay." She shot him a withering glare, as if the impudence of calling on people at mealtimes was more than she could possibly bear.

Dan fell right into the trap, visibly withering and barely able to get out an abject apology. "I'm s—s—so t—terribly sorry for the dreadful inconvenience, Mrs. Butler. I don't need to stay for lunch, I only came for a word with Miss, Doctor, Miss, but—"

"Nonsense!" interrupted Mrs. Butler impatiently. "What kind of people do you think we are that we can't offer a simple meal to a man of the cloth?"

"Mother!" Hannah felt it was time for her to put a stop to Dan's suffering. "Let's all just sit down and eat something." She marched up to the table and sat firmly down in her chair. Her mother and Dan followed.

"Please say the blessing, Mr. Williams," said Mrs. Butler in a businesslike fashion.

"Thank You, Lord Jesus, for the hospitality and graciousness of Mrs. Butler and her daughter. Thank You for the food You have set before us. May it serve to make us strong to enable us to serve You day by day. In the name of Jesus Christ, we pray. Amen."

Hannah raised her eyes and looked at Dan, whose eyes were still closed as though he were not quite finished praying. One day she might actually talk to him about his view of God and ask him why his faith was so different from what she saw at church. But not today. She thought of Rosie and the charm around her neck. There were still some things she needed to sort out about what she truly believed in.

"Well, Mr. Williams," began Mrs. Butler as soon as lunch was finished being served, "I suppose you have heard all the news about the war out there on that mission of yours."

"Yes, indeed," mumbled Dan, who had unfortunately been caught with a mouthful of ham. He swallowed quickly and painfully. "That's why I came to talk to your daughter today, despite it being terribly rude of me to intrude like this."

"Yes, of course, news of that import must get through to even the remotest parts of this dark continent. I myself was absolutely shattered when I heard the dreadful story. I was struck dumb, literally struck dumb. Mind you, so were all the rest of our circle, weren't they, Hannah?" Hannah was glad she was only the partial recipient of the lunch hour tirade. Dan glanced over at her like a cornered animal, and Hannah wondered if he would ever venture to visit them again.

"You must know our esteemed Reverend Cosgrove?" Dan nodded, his mouth unfortunately full again, but it didn't matter. Mrs. Butler went on to give a blow-by-blow account of the morning's sermon.

Hannah looked out and watched Sophie tasting the trees at the edge of the lawn. She hoped her mother wouldn't notice, but she needn't have worried. Mrs. Butler had barely paused to take a breath in the last ten minutes. Her ham and potato salad lay almost untouched. Dan was already finished and pushing a lone potato around his plate trying to pretend he hadn't really wolfed down his meal so fast. Hannah finished her lunch and nodded to Juma, who was standing by the door. Juma came and took away their plates. Mrs. Butler waved hers away also, commenting how it was impossible for her to eat much of anything at a time like this. Juma brought little bowls of custard for each of them and when they were finished, Mrs. Butler stood up, announcing that she was extremely tired and would lie down.

"I didn't expect guests this afternoon and I planned to rest, so you will excuse me, if you don't mind," she announced. Dan blushed and stood up so suddenly his chair fell over backwards. Mrs. Butler glared quickly at Hannah while Dan rushed back to retrieve his chair from the floor.

"Th–thank you so much for you hospitality, Mrs. Butler, I do appre—"

"Don't mention it," Mrs. Butler cut him off and swept back through the door into the house.

Dan sank down into his chair and Hannah heard him

suppress a sigh of relief. She felt so sorry for him and her guilty feelings were exacerbated by her use of him as a foil for her mother this afternoon. She apologized for Mrs. Butler's rudeness. "She hasn't much patience with anyone from a lower social sphere than herself," Hannah explained.

Dan didn't respond. They sat in silence for a few minutes watching Sophie, who was now rolling on the grass, rubbing her back into the ground and making funny little grunting noises.

"She's such a sweet little creature," Hannah broke the silence. "It must be a great joy for you to have her."

"Yes, I have enjoyed her immensely," replied Dan. He looked shyly at Hannah, who smiled pleasantly back at him. Why was it so easy for her to feel at ease with this man while Garth Whitehead threw her into a state of nerves the likes of which she had never experienced before? *Probably because I'm in love with Garth, while I'm not in love with Dan,* she decided.

"I want to talk to you about Sophie, actually," Dan was saying. There was a long pause.

"Please, go on," Hannah prompted.

"It's because of the war."

"Oh no, not the war again!" Hannah groaned. "If I hear any more about that blessed war, I'll just scream!"

"Oh dear, I'm terribly sorry, I didn't mean to bring it up. Perhaps this visit was not a very good plan, Miss Butler." Dan started to push his chair out. Quickly, without thinking what she was doing, Hannah reached out and put her hand on his arm to stop him.

"No, I didn't mean it; please stay! I was just grumbling because of my mother."

Dan stopped instantly, looked at her hand, and turned brilliantly red. Hannah quickly removed it. "Go on, please;

what did you need to ask me?"

Dan took a deep breath. "I feel it is my duty to enlist in the army, Miss Butler, and to serve my country in its time of need. I am going to return to England."

"Oh!" Hannah was taken aback. She had never pictured Dan as a soldier; he was so timid. "What will you do with your mission? What will you do with Sophie?" she blurted in surprise.

"Yes, that is the difficulty. Sophie, I mean, not the mission. I work with Reverend MacRae. He is an elderly gentleman and past the age of soldiering. He will gladly hold the fort, as he puts it, until I am back. But he doesn't want the trouble of Sophie. He thinks wild animals belong in the wild, not in a mission station. So I was wondering," Dan paused and took a deep breath as if to steel himself for the worst, "I was just thinking that you might consider, if it wouldn't be too much trouble, looking after her for me while I am gone. Please don't feel obligated to say yes, if it would be too much of an inconvenience. I wouldn't be at all offended, and I would understand completely." He stopped speaking suddenly and looked desperately at Hannah.

Hannah wanted to reach out and touch his arm again, but instead she just nodded. "Of course, I will. I would love to look after her! It would be my pleasure!" Hannah watched the relief well up in Dan's eyes.

"Oh, Miss Butler, thank you very much! Are you sure it wouldn't be too much trouble for you? They do say we'll be home by Christmas. Of course, it may take longer, but not much longer, I'm sure."

"Don't worry, Mr. Williams, she'll be welcome here as long as you are away. My only worry is for you. What if something should happen to you? War is a dangerous business, or so I've heard."

"Yes, I've heard that too." He smiled ruefully. "But I must do my duty for my God and my country, come what may. I am ready to die. Sophie is the only creature I would leave here on this earth with regret. Yet if anything should happen to me, perhaps you would be so kind as to keep her until she is old enough to return to the wild. I realize it is a lot to request, Miss Butler, but I don't know what else I could do. I must trust that our Lord knows what will be best for us. After all, not a sparrow dies without Him knowing and caring, so I'm sure Sophie's life is safe in His hands also." *And your life, too,* Hannah added to herself.

But there was one thing she must clarify before this agreement went much further. "There is only one thing, Mr. Williams. It is just that my faith in God is not at all like yours. Although I admire your faith and your convictions very much, I find that I do not have the same faith in the Lord's control of the outcome of our lives that you do. I hope that will not be a difficulty for you in leaving Sophie with me should anything happen to you. I would probably just raise her as best as I could and release her into the wild again. What God would have to do with it, I wouldn't know."

"Yes, I have sensed that you are not a Christian, Miss Butler, at least not yet. Nevertheless, you are a compassionate and kind person, and you have a love of nature and God's creatures. Even if you don't yet know God, He knows you and loves you. I'm sure one day you will love Him in return."

Hannah felt skeptical about this. He didn't know that she was wearing a magic charm. It made her feel a little ashamed. Perhaps if he did know, he wouldn't trust her with Sophie. But she tried to put the thought out of her mind.

"Then I'm sure everything will be fine. Sophie will stay

with me and you'll be home by Christmas. It's a bargain!"

She put out her hand, and Dan took it, smiling warmly. "Thank you so much, Miss Butler. You have no idea how much this means to me to have you looking after Sophie while I am gone. The war will be much easier for me knowing that she is in such good hands."

Hannah and Dan rose from the table and walked down the steps of the veranda. Sophie came charging over to greet them, and they bent down to play with her. Dan and Sophie wrestled and tumbled on the grass for a moment while Hannah watched, entranced. What kind of a man was this who was so awkward and shy with people, yet wasn't afraid to look like a fool playing on the grass with a baby elephant? The handsome face of Garth popped into her mind, and she couldn't imagine him even thinking of behaving so foolishly. But, on the other hand, Dan was a kind man, even if he was rather embarrassingly fanatic about that faith of his, not to mention a bit of a fool over this little elephant. Perhaps if it weren't for that faith issue—but no, she was in love with Garth and always would be.

five

Hannah was busy making rounds the following morning, but her mind was elsewhere, as usual. She was with Garth in the distant, misty, unreal future. Mechanically, she went through the motions of her business and was surprised when she was handed a note on a folded piece of familiar fresh white paper. She unfolded it, her heart suddenly pounding in her ears.

"Han, old chap," she read, "King has gone off his feed. Could you please come and look at him as soon as possible? Yours, Garth."

She told the young farmer who was with her that his cow had mastitis and explained the treatment as quickly as she could. She rushed out to Kindye and galloped down the road, leaving a cloud of dust to settle slowly in her wake.

She heard Garth before she saw him, ranting and raving at his horseboy for not telling him soon enough about the horse's trouble. Hannah dismounted and walked quickly into the stables. As her eyes adjusted from the brightness outside, she could hear the boy trying to explain.

"But, Bwana, you were not home last night. We waited for you and sent a toto to fetch you at the country club, but no one there knew where you were."

"Well, then, you should have looked harder!" Garth whirled around and saw Hannah standing in the entrance. "Hannah! There you are. These ignorant Africans have let King get sick. I think he's got blackwater. I hope we're not too late to save him. Come here and tell me what you think can be done."

Hannah's eyes were adjusted to the darkness now, and she could see into King's stall. He had already gone down and was lying panting on the straw. Once a horse was down, there was very little she could do but watch him die. She should have been called in much sooner. She looked at Garth's face. It wasn't the anger in it that took her aback. It was the grayness of the skin and his bloodshot eyes. His hair was unbrushed and his shirt was rumpled and unbuttoned. He looked ghastly. She glanced at the unfortunate horseboy, who was trying to sidle out of the stall under the cover of Hannah's arrival. He looked pleadingly back at her and she nodded quickly, letting him go.

Turning back to Garth, she asked, "How long has he been down? Was he alright yesterday?"

Garth pressed his fingertips to the sides of his temples and groaned. "I don't know." He spoke through clenched teeth. "I wasn't here and those blithering idiots I pay to be horseboys didn't even try to get hold of me. Anyone could have told them I was at Lord Dunbar's over at Lake Navasha, but did they have the sense to ask anyone? It appears not."

Hannah glanced around. The horseboy had disappeared. She bent over and stroked King's mane. Already his breathing had become shallower. He wouldn't last long now. "Why didn't they call me if they couldn't find you?" she asked.

"They said I had given them instructions not to call you unless it was serious. I didn't want to be paying unnecessary fees every time one of the horses sneezed. But no matter how much I explain things to these oafs, they just don't understand horses. They are the most thickheaded, unteachable lot of dunderheads I have ever come across. Why I ever thought Africa was the land of the future, I'll never know. I must have been out of my mind to try to make a living here. I tell you, Hannah, they have driven me to drink."

Hannah doubted it. Even with the sympathy she felt for him, she knew better than that. She knelt down beside King and stroked his huge face, his sensitive ears, and whispered to him comfortingly. Garth paced back and forth, complaining. About three-quarters of an hour later, King finally stopped breathing.

Hannah put her head down and rested it on his mane for a moment. What a magnificent creature he had been. She thought of him pounding around the track just a few short weeks ago, his muscles rippling, his hooves flying, and his huge head straining and pushing forward, willing his body to fly faster. If any creature could be invincible, King was. Yet death had managed to overcome him so easily, so quickly, so irretrievably. He had been powerless.

When Hannah raised her head, she found Garth kneeling beside her. He had come over so quietly, she hadn't noticed. She looked into his eyes and saw tears spill over onto his cheeks. Quickly he covered his eyes with his hand, and they knelt silently together over the great animal's body, and for a moment Hannah thought Garth could have been praying. But she knew better than that, though Dan would have prayed at a time like this. She remembered how he had prayed for Sophie's health. He believed God loved animals. *Please take King's soul to be with You, God, if he does indeed have one.* Hannah whispered the prayer in her heart.

As she prayed, she heard Garth standing up. She struggled stiffly to her feet also. She was cramped with kneeling for so long and with the tension of watching a great creature die. She felt shy to look up into Garth's face again and encounter his grief, but he spoke in a matter-of-fact voice.

"Let's go inside and get some coffee. I could use a cup, and I'd be grateful for your company also." Hannah felt her heart leap into her throat. He had actually asked her to be with him at a time like this. She must mean something to him. She looked up at him, but his face only betrayed a grim resignation. He had managed to master his feelings so quickly.

"Thanks, a coffee would be lovely." She smiled back. She really was getting a little better at talking to him. Perhaps it was the practice she was getting chatting with Dan.

They walked back to Garth's house together. It was a beautiful old place he had bought from one of the founding families of Kikuru. It had a quiet, wide veranda with vines hanging down from the roof and bright-tissue bougainvilleas growing up to meet them. Hannah realized that for all the times she had been to Garth's place, this was the first time she had ever been into his home. The veranda was set comfortably with wicker furniture, but they walked right inside through the large wooden front doors and into a wide, dark room with shiny parquet floors. The furniture inside was definitely bachelor style. The chairs were animal hides strung over wooden frames, the kind you could buy at the bazaar in Nairobi. There were a couple of African drums made of skin tightly stretched over a cylinder and secured with strings pulling painfully downward. There was an elephant foot, stuffed and used as a footstool. Hannah thought of Sophie's feet waving wildly as she rolled on the grass with Dan and winced at the thought of cutting them off. An assortment of wild game trophies, mainly bucks, with horns of various configurations, decorated the walls. Scattered between the hunting trophies were horse rosette ribbons, the only color in the room. But Garth didn't linger here either.

They marched out of the lounge and through a dining room, whose main feature was a heavy oak sideboard stacked with bottles and crystal glasses. From the dining room they went into the kitchen. The cook was sitting on a stool chatting with one of the farm bibis, who was leaning against a door that led outside to the yard. An old dog lay at his feet and only raised its head sleepily when Garth and Hannah entered. The cook stood slowly up.

"*Jambo,* Bwana," he said, looking at Hannah curiously.

"Kamau, get us some coffee on the veranda, will you?" Garth spoke in Swahili, then turned and steered Hannah back into the dining room and through another door to a room with a washstand and washbasin in it. "Would you like to wash up a bit? I'll meet you out on the veranda. I'm just going to get something for this infernal headache I have."

Hannah washed and made her way outside again. There were two wicker chairs with comfortable cushions and a table between them. The table had a pile of books and papers on them. This was obviously where Garth spent most of his time when he was at home. Hannah sat in one of the chairs and looked out at the view. The house was set a little bit up the hill on one side of the valley, and it looked out over the river meandering into town, and the dark green trees interspersed with red tile and silver tin roofs of Kikuru. Beyond the town misty, blue-green hills faded into the dusty blue sky.

After a few minutes, Garth still hadn't appeared, and Hannah looked at the books piled beside her on the table. They were mainly about raising horses, which didn't surprise her much. On the bottom of the pile a letter stuck out as if it had been stuffed under the books to keep it from blowing away in the breeze. "With much love and worry from your Mother," the letter announced in a spidery handwriting. *Of course Garth has a mother,* Hannah thought, surprised because she had never thought of her before. It was common knowledge that he received money from home, and she supposed that of course it must come, at least partly, from his mother.

The house was quiet. Hannah wondered how long Garth would take to find something for his headache. She leaned over the table a little. She thought she'd just look at the last sentence of the letter. Maybe it would tell why his mother was worried about Garth. She felt her face flushing with guilt, but her curiosity was too much for her. She had to at least glance.

"War or no war, I'll be arriving on the next boat to see for myself what you're up to," the letter said. Reading it was so easy. She could just be looking at it by accident. After all, the letter was right out in the open. Hannah leaned over a little more.

"I need to be certain you are not gambling it away," the line above that read, and, "Even here in England I hear rumors about your wild adventures and extravagant ways." This was too much temptation for Hannah to resist. Garth was nowhere nearby. Hannah peered into the dark window of the lounge behind her. All was quiet. She leaned over a little more. There were only three or four lines left sticking out from under the books that she hadn't read.

"You are, after all, thirty-five years old and it is high time you learned how to be responsible. I am on the point of insisting you find a nice quiet girl and settle down to have a family before I send you any more money."

The door burst open and Garth came out carrying a tray of coffee things. Hannah jerked herself quickly back into her chair. She fiddled distractedly with her hat that she had in her lap, not daring to look up at Garth in case he noticed how red her face was and read the guilt in her eyes. But he wasn't paying any attention. His black mood prevented him from noticing anything but his own inconveniences.

"Kamau is one of the laziest, most useless Africans on the whole estate. I can't imagine what Lady Higgins-Smythe thought she was doing when she recommended him to me when I bought the house. If I had any sense, I'd fire the old coot on the spot. But I don't have time to go chasing around after another useless African and then train him on top of that! Cream?" He handed Hannah a china cup and then a dainty pitcher of cream when she nodded.

"I don't know what I'm doing out here in this barbarous country, anyway," he continued after taking a large gulp of his own coffee. "I thought perhaps I needed a new start where no one knew me and I could make my way on my own. But really, I don't know how anyone is supposed to cope with this place. I should have gone out to Australia instead. There would have been less to cope with. They know how to handle their natives down there." There was an uncomfortable silence while Garth brooded on the unfairness of Africa.

"Well," Hannah started. She hesitated, but reminding herself that he had just lost his best horse and he had told her he needed her company, she plunged in. "I for one am glad you chose Africa." Garth swallowed the coffee he had just sipped and looked at her in surprise. Hannah suddenly felt her old shyness overwhelm her, and she looked down at her hat in her lap.

"Why, Han, old chap, thank you. I didn't know. . ." Hannah could feel his eyes looking at her with a new kind of curiosity. "I'll be. . .!" she heard him say a mild curse more to himself than her, and she glanced quickly up at him. He was smiling at her.

"You know, Han, it has been a hard row to hoe here, what with sick horses and deadly diseases and useless Africans. You know more than anyone how hard it has been. You've been here with me through thick and thin, helping with the horses and the Africans and the racing and everything. I couldn't have come this far without your help, you know."

Hannah twisted her hat around and around in her hands

and blushed hideously. She had jumped into water that was far, far too deep for her. One part of her wanted to leap up and run to the stables where she had left Kindye. The other part forced her to stay. This was what she had been wishing and begging for all these past weeks. She must stick it out no matter how she felt, and she felt embarrassed beyond belief. Garth was saying nice things to her, but somehow she had imagined it would feel different. Warmer and friendlier, perhaps. Suddenly Garth reached over the table, moved the books out of the way, and took her hand out of her lap. She looked up at him. Nothing was different. He was smiling at her the way he always did, half teasing, half serious. But now he was actually holding her hand. "Thank you, Han, old ch—" He stopped himself midword. "I shouldn't call you that, should I? It really isn't very flattering. I'll have to think of a new name for you. Just give me some time and I'll come up with one!"

This was too much for Hannah. Her shyness overcame her desire. She couldn't banter back and forth with him; in fact, she could hardly say a word. "I must go now, Garth." At least she had managed to say his name. She pulled her hand away and without looking at him, she fled off the veranda and across the lawn.

"Han, what about your coffee? You haven't even touched it." But she was running like a frightened gazelle. "Bye, Han! I'll call on you next week if you don't mind." She was fleeing too desperately to turn around. She jumped onto Kindye and galloped home as if her life depended on it.

For once she was glad to see her mother sitting on the veranda waiting for her. As soon as she caught sight of Hannah, she ordered lunch. By the time Hannah had given Kindye to the syce and washed up, lunch dishes were on the table waiting to be served. Mrs. Butler had a whole morning full of information that she had heard from Harriet Fitzhugh, who had called in for coffee. Hannah sat and picked at her meal in grateful silence, nodding at the appropriate pauses while the news of Kikuru and the war in Europe flowed harmlessly over her head.

Hannah spent that week in a state of turmoil. She didn't sleep well at night. It was too difficult to stop her mind from going over and over the conversation she and Garth had had. When she had exhausted herself replaying every detail and nuance, she imagined how it would be when he came to call on her. She would be wearing a dress, of course. Maybe her green one with the white collar. It was either that or the navy blue one that she always wore to church. But that was too severe; besides, she had worn it to the races. No, it would be the green one, and Garth would look at her with admiration in his eyes the way she had seen him look at Felicity or Leticia that day at the race. He would take her hand in his and raise it to his lips, and she would look up into his eyes. . . .

These daydreams attacked her mind with vengeance now. She could hardly think of anything else. In her heart of hearts she knew that Garth broke hearts the way elephants broke trees, leaving them bare and torn as they went on to greener younger ones just further on. But the more she dreamed of him, the less she remembered what she knew about him. She fingered the little shell she wore around her neck and wished she could live in her daydreams forever.

The week stretched slowly on. Each afternoon, Hannah rode eagerly home from her office, looking for a sign that Garth would be there calling on her. Would she see his horse tied up at the veranda? Would he be sitting having a drink with Mother? Perhaps there would be a message telling when to expect him. Hannah had her green dress ironed and waiting. But the days went by and no one came.

On Friday a letter from Charles came for her. Hannah opened the letter absentmindedly, vaguely wondering why he would write to her so soon. Surely he couldn't have left Mombasa yet. With little interest, she began to read the letter.

> *My dear Hannah,*
>
> *I am awaiting the departure of my ship, which has been delayed for a few days due to the possibility of submarines being in the vicinity, although I personally feel this is very unlikely.*
>
> *It has, however, made me realize how fleeting life can be, especially during times of war. I therefore decided I must write to you and declare my intentions. In case I do not reach England safely, I would like you to know that I have the highest regard for you. I fear that I may even be in love with you. If you have any feelings for me at all (I rather hope that you do), I would be most grateful if you would let me know. It would make my separation from you almost bearable if you were to inform me that I may live in hope of a happy reunion after the war. In short, Hannah, I am asking you to consider being my wife. You need not decide right away, I only ask that you tell me if there is any hope that you can love me. I look forward to hearing from you at your earliest possible convenience.*
>
> *With deepest regards,*
> *Charles*

Hannah quickly folded the letter. Her first thought was that she must not let her mother see this. Mrs. Butler was sitting opposite her at the table, watching her read the letter with great interest. Hannah knew her mother felt she must take charge of Hannah's relationship with Charles, since Hannah herself was so incapable of doing it properly.

"Well, Hannah, what did he say? Why did he write so soon? He must be very interested in keeping in touch with you to write so soon. What did he say?"

"Nothing," Hannah lied. "He was delayed in Mombasa because of a submarine scare and he was just passing the time in writing letters, that's all." But Hannah's telltale cheeks were pink, and Mrs. Butler obviously wasn't satisfied.

"Give it to me to see, dear. A man doesn't write to a woman just to pass time. I know far more about these things than you do. Let me see the letter." She held out her hand, but Hannah knew she would have no peace if her mother knew that Charles had proposed to her. She must not let her have it.

&

On Sunday she wore the green dress to church with her mother, who complained that it was too frivolous to wear to the Lord's house. Hannah ignored her and looked out instead for Fiona. But Fiona wasn't there. They rode home together in the buggy discussing which men were heading back to England to sign up. War was declared, but there was no fighting as of yet. Just armies gathering around Europe. The world seemed to be holding its breath. Garth wouldn't be going, Hannah knew. She wondered if his mother would be arriving soon. She had hoped to find out from Fiona.

When they drove up the track to their house, Hannah's heart leaped. There on the veranda stood a man. Garth!

No, it wasn't Garth. Hannah glanced sheepishly at her mother to see if she had noticed the sudden joy in her face when she had seen the man. But her mother hadn't noticed him yet. *It must be Dan,* Hannah thought as they approached. She felt angry and betrayed. Why did he have to come today of all days? And right at lunchtime, of course! What if Garth arrived and he was there? She must find a way to get rid of him.

"Mother, look, Mr. Williams is on the veranda. Do you really think we need to invite him to lunch with us again?" Hannah felt mean-spirited and unkind. Really, she did like Dan Williams, but he was just so. . .so. . .inconvenient.

Mrs. Butler glanced at her daughter in mild surprise. "I thought you enjoyed Mr. Williams's company. But it wouldn't upset me just to mention that I am not feeling well. After all, he could at least send us word ahead of time if he wants to show up on our doorstep every Sunday." The syce pulled the horse to a halt in front of the veranda, and Dan stepped forward to hand Mrs. Butler and Hannah down.

"Good afternoon, Mr. Williams," said Mrs. Butler firmly as she alighted on the ground. "I am afraid I am not well this afternoon," she began. But Dan was looking up at Hannah in the buggy. He reached up to take her hand, and as he did so she looked down into his eyes. There was the look she had been imagining in Garth's eyes all week. His eyes followed her as she stepped down and just before he let go of her hand, he whispered, "You—you—look so nice today, Miss Butler." Then he turned hopelessly red and stared at the ground.

Mrs. Butler was still speaking. "So, Mr. Williams, if you don't mind excusing us today, we will have to dine alone."

"I am terribly sorry to intrude, Mrs. Butler. I–I—just mentioned last week to Miss Butler that I would be bringing Sophie over before I shipped out. She very kindly offered to look after her for me. I'll just leave her here and be on my way, if you would be so good as to excuse me."

"Oh, dear, I didn't expect you would be leaving so soon, Mr. Williams!" Hannah interrupted. "I thought it would be a matter of weeks, not a matter of days!"

"I'm terribly sorry, I should have explained more carefully. Please forgive me. If it is inconvenient for me to leave Sophie with you, I will take her back with me and leave her at my mission. It was frightfully remiss of me not to explain to you exactly when I was leaving. There is a merchant freighter shipping out of Mombasa for Southampton in three days. I have managed to secure a berth on it as I am anxious to get back and enlist as soon as I possibly can."

"Oh, don't worry about Sophie, she's very welcome to stay with me," Hannah explained quickly to save Dan from any more apologies. Secretly she wondered how he was planning to fight for his country when he could barely face her without crumbling with fear. A man like Garth, on the other hand, she could see marching handsomely and confidently off to war with Charles Montague, but of course Garth wasn't going unless it was absolutely necessary. She found herself admiring Dan, but quickly she pushed the thought away. Garth would probably be coming over any minute. After all, he had probably been waiting all week to come over on Sunday when she wasn't working. She must get rid of Dan.

Suddenly Sophie noticed that Hannah was there and she ambled up to say hello. "Hello, Sophie," said Hannah, stroking her between the eyes. "I hope you're going to be happy here. We'll take very good care of you until your master gets home from fighting in the war." She turned to Dan. "Come around to the stables with me and we'll settle Sophie in before you head home. You must be anxious to get back. I suppose you have a lot to do before you leave." She felt mean and unkind again. It was amazing what the expectation of a visit from Garth could drive her to. She knew it would be hard for Dan to say good-bye to Sophie, and it was very selfish of her to make him do it so quickly. But Dan followed her gratefully to the stables.

She picked her way carefully over the hay and the dirt of the stable floor because she hadn't wanted to change from church. She led Sophie into a clean, empty stall and called a stableboy to cover the floor with straw. She discussed Sophie's feeding arrangements with the syce, and she and Dan headed back toward the farmhouse. Hannah was relieved to see that there was no sign of either Garth or his horse yet.

When they reached the front lawn, Dan knelt down to say good-bye to the little elephant. She thought he was bending down to play with her, and she put her trunk around his neck and pulled him onto the grass. "Oh, Sophie girl, I'll miss you so much," Dan said as they rolled together. "You be a good girl now until I get back for you. Don't cause any trouble for Hannah. . .Miss Butler, I mean." He buried his face in Sophie's ear so that Hannah couldn't see his embarrassment. But he didn't take it out. Sophie lay panting on the grass and when Dan finally looked up, Hannah was touched and ashamed to see that his eyes were filled with tears.

He stood up and reached shyly out to shake Hannah's hand. He had the musty smell of elephant on him and he didn't meet Hannah's eyes. "Thank you, Miss Butler; it means so much to me, all you are doing for Sophie."

"Please, it will be my pleasure to have her. We'll get along just fine, won't we, Sophie?" Sophie was trying to pull Dan back down onto the grass with her trunk.

"Would it be alright if I wrote to you now and then, Miss Butler? I am afraid I will miss everything so much and it would be awfully good of you if you could write back to me now and then with news of Sophie, if it wouldn't be too much trouble."

"Of course, I'd be happy to write and tell you all Sophie's news. And it would be good to hear from you too," she added quickly as an afterthought. After all, the poor man was going off to war.

"Good-bye, Miss Butler. Good-bye, Sophie girl." Dan turned and quickly strode down the driveway. Sophie started to follow him, but Hannah stopped her. She bent down and held her around the neck. Dan turned and looked quickly over his shoulder, and Hannah saw him take out a handkerchief and blow his nose. Sadly, she led Sophie back to the house.

six

The little elephant was distraught when Dan left. She kept trying to run down the driveway as if he were waiting just around the corner for her. Hannah's heart went out to her, so she sat with her on the stoop and comforted her all afternoon. She scratched behind Sophie's ears and stroked her between her eyes and down her wrinkly trunk. Whenever she took her hands away, Sophie made a break for the driveway to follow the sad figure of Dan walking alone and lonely. But Hannah's eyes were also searching the driveway. She was sure any minute Garth would appear riding tall and confidently around the bend, handsome and smiling.

Sophie spent a miserable night in the stable, and Hannah could hear her trumpeting forlornly all through the night. The next day, Sophie followed Hannah everywhere, much to the delight of everyone who brought animals to Hannah's clinic. Sophie was quite a little celebrity by the end of the day. All the attention did her good, and she seemed a little happier by the time the two of them trudged up the driveway in the long evening shadows. Hannah had her hand slung companionably over Sophie's short wrinkly neck. Sophie no longer whimpered and tried to run away down the driveway. She seemed to accept Hannah as a reasonable substitute for Dan and as long as Hannah was nearby, she was content.

Hannah took her straight to the stables and fed her her supper. She could tell Sophie was exhausted from her wakeful night and her busy day. She closed her into the little stall, and Sophie barely complained before she was quiet and, Hannah assumed, asleep.

It was dark when Hannah reached the farmhouse.

"I had supper without you," called Mrs. Butler from the veranda where she sat with a small lamp flickering bravely against the huge dark night.

"Good," said Hannah, "I was just getting Sophie settled. I'll go and eat, then I'm turning in. I didn't get much sleep last night."

Hannah was grateful for her tiredness. The thought of Garth flicked across her mind as she dropped her head on her soft welcoming pillow, and she wondered what he was doing tonight. But she had hardly given him a thought all day because she had had her hands and mind full with Sophie. She was asleep before she gave him another thought.

≈

Sophie and Hannah became inseparable as the weeks passed. The little elephant grew happy and playful again. Children would come down from the compounds of the surrounding farms just to see her and play with her, and Sophie lapped up all the attention like it was ice cream, but only as long as Hannah was nearby. She always had one eye on her, and the minute Hannah went out of sight, Sophie stopped whatever she was doing and slipped away after her. Hannah got so used to her being underfoot that she hardly noticed her anymore when she was working.

The only one who didn't fall in love with Sophie was Simba. Simba didn't appreciate being followed around by an elephant. Hannah was sure she felt it was beneath her dignity to be trailed by such a shuffling, baggy-skinned, long-nosed creature. Every time Sophie passed near her, Simba would give a low growl so Hannah could see just how unfair it was for her to be forced to mingle with such an unhorselike little thing. Sophie, unfortunately, thought it was some sort of a game, and she lifted her trunk and trumpeted gleefully into Simba's face. Simba would get up and turn her back to her in disgust. "Simba, you ridiculous old thing," Hannah would exclaim. "You're just jealous of a silly elephant!"

Garth did finally come to see Hannah. She was trudging home from delivering a calf late one afternoon, dirty and weary. Sophie, who was following along behind Kindye, was the first to notice him cantering up from behind them. She trumpeted a friendly greeting, and Hannah turned to see him. While her heart jumped with joy for a moment, her stomach sank as she realized what she looked like. Quickly, she pulled her hat down over her damp, greasy hair and wiped her forehead and cheeks with her sleeve because she could feel the dirt and grime that had settled on her face as she worked on the cow. She wiped her hands on her trousers just as Garth caught up to her.

"Han, old chap, long time no see. What have you been doing with yourself these days? Working too hard as usual, I suspect." Hannah blushed as his eyes took in her appearance and he seemed to laugh inwardly. Then he turned to look at Sophie. "I heard rumors about this little addition to your family. What a little charmer she is, too!" Sophie was giving Garth a good once-over with her trunk. He took it as a compliment, of course.

"Yes," Hannah said, "I am looking after Sophie for a friend who is over in England joining up." Did he not realize that he had promised to call on her? Had he completely forgotten everything that had happened on the afternoon King died?

"You are the serious one, aren't you, Han? Joining up, you say. Well, if they ever start anything over there it may be worth it, but from what I hear they're just shouting insults at each other over the trench lines. Some war!" He snorted. "I have better things to do.

"Are you going to be able to help me with the horses this season, Han? I am still devastated without King, but Raj, my three-year-old, is looking awfully well these days. You really must come and have a look at him for yourself. I think you'll be impressed."

"Certainly, if you want me to," Hannah replied, giving Kindye a little kick to move her along. She couldn't believe how Garth could have forgotten their last conversation so easily. He was behaving as if nothing at all had passed between them. And she had been living all these last few weeks on the memory of that conversation—eating, drinking, and dreaming it. Garth followed along cheerfully, oblivious to Hannah's moody reply.

"Wonderful! I am really hoping to have a good season. My mother's coming over on the next boat, you know, and I am determined to impress her. But I am going to need your help to do that. What do you say you drop by tomorrow to have a look at Raj run? Surely you can spare a few minutes from your busy day. These old farmers can deliver their own calves for once in their lives. I need you more than they do." Garth chatted on, quite unaware of Hannah's silence. They came around the bend in the driveway in view of the house and Mrs. Butler on the veranda. Garth reined in his horse.

"Well, I'll be off then, Han, old chap. It's been lovely to chat with you again. See you tomorrow morning!" He turned his horse and clattered off, leaving Hannah and Sophie staring after him. Hannah turned back to the house. Unfortunately, her mother had witnessed the whole scene.

"Hannah Butler, look at you! You look absolutely hideous! How could you possibly leave someone's house looking like that? No wonder Mr. Whitehead didn't come up to the house. He was probably embarrassed to be seen in public with you. You did invite him in, didn't you? Didn't you?"

"He had to go," Hannah mumbled as she handed Kindye off to the syce. She patted Sophie on the rump, so she dutifully trotted off after the syce to get her dinner. Feeling humiliated, Hannah pulled her hat off and slipped past her mother and into the house.

"There's a letter for you," she heard her mother say just before the door slammed behind her. Hannah looked up and there on the mantelpiece a white envelope stood out in the gloom of the shadowy room. *It's from Dan,* she thought as she tore it open. She felt a sliver of gladness pierce her black mood. "It's funny how Dan always manages to appear just when I'm feeling my worst," she said to herself as she walked slowly through the house to her room, reading as she went. He wrote in a fast, confident script, quite unlike how Hannah would have imagined from his stuttering speech.

Dear Hannah,

I have arrived safely in England and everyone here is gearing up for the war, although not much is happening yet. I will be shipping out to France tomorrow and I just wanted to drop you a line before I left.

I miss Africa more than I thought possible. England seems so small and tame and crowded in comparison to our beautiful wild landscapes and huge dramatic skies. I have been thinking of you often and wondering how Sophie is getting along also.

Hannah cringed a little, realizing how little she had been thinking of Dan, her mind being so full of Garth.

I am praying that you are both well and that Sophie is not being too much trouble to you. I thank God every day for your gracious willingness to help me out with her. I know she takes a lot of looking after! Thank you, Hannah.

If you don't mind my writing to you about myself, I am doing fine in every way, except for a severe case of

*homesickness. But should God see fit to spare me from
death, I will be home as soon as the war is over.
Otherwise I will also be home, with Him. I often think
heaven must look like Africa in some ways, but of
course without the disease and the sickness and suffering, not to mention war.*

*I hope I am not imposing on your good will too much,
but I would be grateful if I may write to you about my
feelings and experiences over here. I feel quite alone. I
have come to love Africa in my years of work out there
and I miss it very much. I miss little Sophie also, and if I
may be so bold as to say so I do miss walking over to
visit you and the enjoyable conversations we had. If you
do manage to find the time now and then, I would be
deeply grateful if you could send me a note to let me
know how Sophie is.*

*I must go now. I am praying for a quick, merciful end
to this war, and I am always thanking God for your
friendship and care for God's little creature, Sophie.*

*In Christ's Love,
Dan*

By the time Hannah had finished reading the letter, she
was sitting on the edge of her bed. She put her head into her
hands and prayed, "Dear God, I know You don't hear from
me often, if You exist at all, but I do pray that You would be
so kind as to spare Dan's life in the war and bring him safely
back to his beloved Africa. He believes in You, and although
I don't know what I believe about You, if You are there,
please keep Dan safe. Thank You. Amen."

She sighed deeply and raised her head. Dan himself was
like Africa. He always brought such a wide-open perspective
to her small, narrow thoughts. Here she had been so depressed
about Garth seeing her look so dirty after he hadn't even

come to visit her when he said he would. But Dan was thinking about life and death, war and peace. About Africa and elephants. About her kindness to him, not her appearance. Why couldn't Garth be more like Dan? She shook the thought out of her head. Garth was so much more exciting and charming than Dan. How could she possibly want him to be different?

But she would write back to Dan. After all, they were friends, she did enjoy his company, and he was feeling so homesick. Besides, she needed to tell him that Sophie was doing very well and he needn't worry about her.

"Hannah, hurry up; your supper is getting cold," her mother's voice drifted through the house. Hannah quickly cleaned up and went out to the veranda, where her supper was waiting for her.

She wrote to Dan that very evening and went to bed early. She wanted to get up early in the morning because she was determined that she would go to Garth's house looking her very best.

When Hannah left the house in the morning, her blond hair shone in the clean morning sunshine. She had a clean white shirt and clean trousers, and she looked and felt as fresh as the morning itself. But in Africa even the most beautiful morning can turn into a hot and dusty midday in a matter of minutes.

She had left Sophie behind, bellowing forlornly in the stables with the syce. But she didn't want Sophie frightening Garth's horses. Besides, it was high time Sophie learned that she couldn't go everywhere with her.

Garth was already out in the paddock and the horses were just about ready for their run.

"Aha, Han, old chap, there you are! Just in time, too. I want you to take a look at Raj and tell me what you think of him. I have high hopes for this horse. He may even be as good as King was."

Raj's jockey took him around the paddock several times. When he stopped running, Raj whinnied with impatience and tossed his mane in the air, prancing and stepping nervously. But as soon as he was allowed to run, a look of concentration and intensity came into his eyes and he took off like a rocket, hooves thundering and nostrils flaring. Hannah was impressed.

She looked up at Garth, who was standing at the fence next to her with his hands in his pockets and his cap pulled low over his handsome face. "I think he will do very well, Garth," she said shyly, still awkward about saying his name out loud.

Garth took his eyes off the horse and looked down at Hannah, as if he had only just noticed her. His eyes strayed from her face, down her blouse and trousers, and back up to her face. Hannah blushed. It was gratifying to see the look of appreciation in Garth's eyes when they met hers again, but it was also strangely humiliating to be surveyed like so much horseflesh.

"Well, thank you, Hannah," he said in his most charming voice, and Hannah's heart stopped beating. Garth put his arm around her shoulders and looked out at the horse on the far side of the paddock. "He is a fine runner, isn't he?"

Hannah nodded. "He is indeed," she breathed, too overcome to trust her voice to anything more than a faint whisper. They stood watching Raj come closer and closer along the fence. Like a locomotive at full speed, he roared by. The dust settled over the two of them, and Hannah felt a shiver of pleasure go through Garth's arm over her shoulder. Suddenly, he bent down and kissed her on her lips.

"Hey, you two, what's this kanoodling in broad daylight!" A voice boomed out from behind them, and Hannah turned as if she had just been caught with her hand in the till. But Garth laughed out loud as if he were caught kissing people every day.

"Jim! You old renegade, you! How dare you come creeping up on us like that? I'm liable to turn and shoot you like a thief if you do that to me again." The two men laughed and Jim dismounted from his horse and shook Garth's hand. Hannah then noticed that Fiona was riding along just behind him. But Fiona wasn't laughing. In fact, she looked positively angry as she glared at her husband and Garth.

"Hello, Garth, Hannah," she said without smiling. Hannah smiled up at her and felt a fountain of blood rushing into her face. Fiona dismounted and walked over to the fence. The four of them stood in silence, watching Raj race around the paddock.

"Very nice," Jim said to Garth. The two of them talked about the race coming up next month. Hannah listened as well as she could, but her mind couldn't stop replaying the kiss. Over and over she lived it: the closeness of Garth's eyes looking into hers, the warmth of his lips on hers, the feel of his fingers on her face, and most of all the elation that surged through her body in response to his touch.

Gradually, she sensed something going on around her. Fiona was speaking, arguing. Her harsh voice penetrated into Hannah's consciousness.

"Jim, we simply cannot afford to bet on these horses anymore, and I don't care how good you two think they are. There are always better horses, or the horse stumbles, or the jockey doesn't run him properly, or something. You are driving us into the poorhouse with this gambling of yours. And Garth too. I know you are losing money, Garth. Don't you think I don't hear things! But you have your mother's money to bail you out and we have nothing!" She stopped speaking abruptly, as though she would break down if she said anything else.

"Now, now, darling, you're working yourself into a terrible state about nothing. I'm not putting all our money on

Garth's horses, just a little. And Raj is a sure bet. Just look at him. He's magnificent!" Jim tried to put his arm around his wife's shoulders, but she shook him off and turned to face Hannah.

"Hannah, you know what it's like. Surely you can tell him that animals cannot be relied upon. Anything can happen at the last minute, you must know that. Tell him!"

Hannah was dismayed. How could she get into an argument between a husband and wife? How could she take sides with someone against Garth? She couldn't. She stared helplessly at Fiona, watching as the look in Fiona's eyes turned from pleading to contempt to rage.

"So, you're in this too! I might have known. You know he's just playing along with you, don't you, Hannah? I saw him kissing you when we rode up here. Don't be fooled. He doesn't mean anything. He only cares about himself and his precious money. He goes through women as quickly as he goes through money. He doesn't care whose women or whose money, just as long as he gets what he wants. And he's even got Jim charmed into giving him whatever he wants. Be warned, Hannah Butler!" She marched over to her horse and rode away down the road, leaving Garth, Jim, and Hannah staring after her in shocked silence.

"Well!" said Garth as soon as she had disappeared from sight. "Women!" He turned back to the paddock where his jockey had just dismounted and was rubbing down Raj. "So, do you think we have a chance at the cup next month?"

"I don't think there is another horse in the country that could touch him," Jim responded, as though carrying on a conversation after his wife had just stormed off was the most natural thing in the world to him.

Hannah felt ill. She was fighting off the horrible thought that Fiona might be right about Garth. But of course, Fiona was really angry at her own husband. After all, Jim wasn't as well off as Garth was, and he probably wasn't as clever or as charming as Garth. She probably just found it easier to blame Garth for their problems instead of blaming her own husband.

No, she couldn't blame Garth for Jim's faults. That wasn't fair. And Garth didn't even have the advantage of having a wife to love him. No wonder he invested his whole life in his horses. Hannah understood that feeling. Of course, it wasn't very nice of Garth to have said what he did when Fiona left, but she couldn't really blame him after what Fiona had said about him.

Having settled this in her mind, Hannah turned her attention to the men's conversation. But they were so engrossed in arguing about the merits and faults of the competing horses, they had forgotten she was there. They wandered off toward the stables, and Garth didn't even look over his shoulder to see if she was coming along.

The morning sun had moved up overhead. The air was shimmering over the paddock. Dust seeped into Hannah's skin, and she felt hot and muggy. Her hair was plastered onto her forehead, and she wished she had brought her hat. Vanity—it was all very well in the morning, but it didn't leave a person much protection in the heat of the day. She walked over to where Kindye was grazing on some grass under a thorn tree. She should get back to work, and Sophie didn't like to be left alone for too long.

But as soon as she was on the lonely road home, her mind returned to Garth's kiss. *It's worth living for,* she decided, *no matter what Fiona says.*

Mrs. Butler was waiting anxiously for Hannah on the veranda when she rode up to the house. She gleefully presented her with a letter from Charles. Hannah took it, wondering what he was going to spring on her now, and how she would ever prevent her mother from finding out about his proposal? She opened the letter with nervous fingers.

Dear Hannah,

My regiment is still undergoing training exercises in England. It seems to take so terribly long. However, I hear terrible rumors of the conditions in trenches in Europe. And they say the Germans are using gas! I shudder to think that it is true!

I hope you received my last letter and have given some thought to your feelings for me. I look so forward to hearing from you to know whether I might dare to hope. I pray that the powers that be will protect me from any permanent injury so that I may return to you after the war as a suitable husband for you. And I pray also that the war will be over soon, but I fear it may last longer than we all thought.

With my highest regards,
Charles

Hannah looked up from the letter into the excited face of her mother eagerly watching her from across the lunch table.

"Well, what did he say? How is he, and is the war going to be over soon? Did he say anything about his feelings for you? A man doesn't write so often unless he has feelings, you know, my dear. I know these things. Tell me; what did he say?"

Hannah sighed and prepared a careful white lie for her mother. "He is still engaged in training, Mother, so he has time to write, that's all. But he feels that the war may last longer than we thought it would, and he hears rumors that the Germans are using gas on the soldiers in the trenches."

She sat back, pleased to see the horror on her mother's face at the mention of gas. That would distract her from prying into Charles's feelings for her.

❧

"The British Army has begun fighting in Europe!" Mrs.

Butler was reading the morning paper agitatedly at the breakfast table a few days later. "The Germans have invaded Belgium, and they are pushing their way into France!"

"Oh dear!" replied Hannah, sitting down. "I hope Dan will be alright." But Hannah's mind was far away from Europe and Dan. Her inner thoughts were only of Garth, but she had no intention of discussing them with her mother, so she listened with one ear as her mother read her the news.

The racing season would be starting again soon, and Hannah wanted to make sure Garth had Raj on the best possible diet. She thought she would pop over to his place after she had finished at the clinic that morning. Absentmindedly, she pushed her chair out from the table and excused herself. Her mother stopped in midsentence to look at her, but then she continued reading as though Hannah were still there.

It is a strange thing, Hannah thought to herself as she walked down the driveway with Sophie following happily along behind her, *how two women can live together in the same house and have absolutely no idea what is going on in the mind or the heart of the other one.* She shuddered at the thought of sharing her inmost thoughts with her mother. *Well, perhaps it's just as well.*

Sophie followed her to Garth's later that morning. She caused quite a sensation in the stables. The syces and stableboys all wanted to see her and touch her. Hannah found herself thinking of Dan as she explained Sophie to them. Perhaps he was already involved in the fighting. She stroked Sophie behind her ears and bent her head forward and whispered a prayer that Dan's God would be gracious enough to keep him safe and bring him home soon, for Sophie's sake.

Garth came striding into the stable and stopped short at the sight of Sophie. Remembering that he had seen her at Hannah's, he laughed and stroked her trunk. Hannah straightened up and put out her hand.

"Good morning, Garth," she said, blushing warmly. He took her hand and greeted her with a peck on the cheek.

"Han, old chap, what brings you here?" He appeared not to notice her red face, nor did he seem to remember the kiss from the day before.

"Well," Hannah stumbled over her words, "I just. . .well. . . it seems that I ought to make sure that Raj's diet is adequate for all the training he is going to do for the upcoming races."

"But of course, my dear; I'll just let you speak to the syce about that. I have to run. Did I tell you my mother is coming out to visit me? I hear she'll be arriving on the day before the Kikuru Cup. What timing! I think I'll throw a party for her arrival and introduce her to the neighbors after the race. You'll come, of course?"

"Y–yes, if you like." Hannah couldn't believe her ears. It had actually happened at last. He had invited her to a party at his house. She was suddenly overwhelmed with shyness. How would she manage it? She had always been so terribly awkward at social do's. She pulled her hat down over her eyes.

"Of course I like! And bring your mother along too. I'll send out formal invitations as soon as I'm organized. Here's Jomo! Tell him exactly what you think Raj should be eating. I must run. Cheerio!" And he turned and was gone.

Hannah had to make an enormous effort to control her thoughts. They had flown out the door with Garth, and she could hardly rein them in so that she could focus on Raj's diet. There was so much else to think through. She was actually invited to one of Garth's parties. That said something about how he felt about her. And what about what she would wear and how she would behave, and whether Garth would pay attention to her in front of all his friends, even his mother? Raj's diet was so hard to think about at a time like this. It was only with a supreme effort that she was able to pull herself together and do her job.

∂•

"Hello, Hannah; you're late again." Hannah's mother was sitting at the table on the veranda when Hannah wandered dreamily up the driveway, still lost in daydreams of Garth and trailed by Sophie. "There's a letter here for you from that Dan Williams fellow. I completely forgot to give it to you this morning. I was so upset about the news from Europe."

"Thanks," Hannah said, taking it and absentmindedly opening it. "Garth Whitehead has invited us to a party at his house on the day of the Kikuru Cup. His mother will be here then and he is throwing a party to welcome her."

"Oh, my goodness gracious me!" Mrs. Butler let her knife and fork fall onto her plate with a clatter. "What will you wear? You have nothing at all. Nothing whatsoever! We must go to Nairobi. And everything I have is old and tired. I'll have to have something made as well.

"Oh, my goodness! Imagine, an invitation to one of Garth Whitehead's parties. It must be because I invited him for lunch when you brought him over to see the horses. He finally realizes that despite your rough appearance, we are people of quality. Oh, dear, there is so much to do, and so little time to do it!" Mrs. Butler began fanning herself distractedly with her napkin.

Hannah looked down at the letter she was holding.

Dear Hannah,

I was so gratified to get your letter yesterday while I was here in France. You have no idea how much it cheered me up to hear how well you and Sophie are getting along. I could almost smell the African air in between the pages.

I am writing to you from what they call a trench. We live like moles in the ground here, and every time it rains we are waist deep in mud. But the worst of it is the

*incoming shellfire and rumors of soldiers being gassed
in the trenches. We fire at the Germans and they retali-
ate. Day and night it goes on, and you never know when
your particular section of the trench will be hit.*

*There isn't much chance of surviving if you take a
direct hit, but so far God has graciously spared my
life. Just yesterday, I had a very close call. I was sitting with my unit playing cards to pass the time when
suddenly I had an overwhelming urge to walk. My
comrades thought I was balmy, but I couldn't sit still. I
got up and made my way through the trench towards
where the next unit was holding the line, when suddenly I heard the whistle of incoming fire. I turned just
in time to see the spot where my friends had been sitting take a direct hit. Rushing back to where I was
only moments ago, all I found were the stumps of my
comrades' legs. I dropped to my knees and prayed. I
only hope that I will be worthy to serve God in whatever capacity He has spared my life for. I don't deserve
to be alive today.*

Hannah looked up with unseeing eyes. Her mother was
still chattering excitedly about the upcoming party. Or was it
the raging war in Europe? Whatever it was, it didn't really
matter to her as long as she could be in a state of alarm over
it. Hannah wasn't listening anyway. She wondered if Garth
would decide to return to England to serve his country now
that things were getting so serious. She thought of the
stumps of Dan's friends' legs and hoped Garth wouldn't be
so foolish as to risk his life unnecessarily. After all, Dan had
God protecting him. Who would protect Garth?

❧

The weeks passed with excruciating slowness. Hannah and
her mother made the necessary trips to Nairobi, and Hannah

was fitted for a gorgeous brown silk dress with an off-the-shoulder bodice and a full skirt. The color complimented her hair and brought out its red highlights while the style emphasized her thin waist, so the dressmaker explained. Hannah hardly recognized herself when she finally tried on the finished product. It literally took her breath away to see herself standing in the looking glass, tall and willowy and feminine. She could sweep Garth off his feet in a dress like this. And right then and there while staring at her own image, she made a vow.

I will get him. Whatever it takes, that is what I will do. The highest mountain; I'll climb it. The deepest river; I'll swim it. The wildest animal; I'll tame it. Garth Whitehead, you don't stand even the ghost of a chance. Come what may, you will be mine! She smiled sweetly at herself, then turned away to change back into her old clothes.

When Hannah arrived home that day, there were letters from Charles and Dan. She opened Charles's letter first. Charles wrote to her regularly. Every letter he wrote to her seemed to give him more confidence that she must accept his proposal. She evaded the issue in her return letters.

She had been writing regularly to Dan to keep him updated on Sophie's growth and antics. She liked to tell him how Sophie followed her nearly everywhere she went these days. All the farmers that she visited expected Sophie now, and they loved to talk to her and treat her with little tidbits that they would save when they knew Hannah would be coming.

Hannah opened Dan's letter. It was short. All it said was that he was too tired to write much. They were in Belgium, near the city of Ypres, and the fighting was brutal and unrelenting.

We still get mail now and then, and the letters I get from you give me the strength to go on. Thank you, and please pray for me and all the soldiers. We are hanging on by only a thread these days. If I don't come home again, thank you for taking such good care of Sophie. It gives me immense comfort to know she is in your capable hands. My prayers are with you.

With love from Dan

Hannah hung her head after she had read the letters. If either of them knew how very little she thought of them these days, she would be so ashamed. She dutifully wrote each week, but other than that, Dan Williams and Charles Montague barely crossed her mind. "Oh, Lord God," she prayed with a guilty heart, "please look after Dan and Charles and all the men fighting in the Great War. Help them to victory quickly. And please bring Dan safely back to Africa, which he loves so much." She folded the letter. She didn't mention Charles's return. There would be terribly awkward scenes when he got back. She wanted to pray that he would somehow stay in England forever, but she didn't know if that was the right kind of prayer to pray. Luckily, Dan was different, although lately she had caught herself thinking that if she didn't know better, she could imagine that Dan had feelings for her. But she quickly put the thought out of her mind. Perhaps she would be with Garth by the time Dan came back.

She was seeing a lot of Garth these days. It was the racing season, and Garth was racing his horses in several different places around the country. Hannah kept his horses in "fighting trim" as he called it, so she was often over at his place overseeing their feed and exercise as well as their general health. The weeks breezed happily past for Hannah. No matter where Garth spent his evenings, she knew he would be spending his days with her and his beloved horses.

seven

By the time the day of the Kikuru Cup finally dawned, Hannah had fingered the little cowrie shell around her neck that Rosie had given her almost bare. She kept it with her wherever she went, and every time she thought about Garth, she touched it. She hadn't seen much of Garth in the last few days. He had been busy preparing for his mother's arrival, so he usually just left a message with his syce for Hannah. She had seen Jim and Fiona at the farm a few times, but Fiona deliberately avoided her. Usually, though, Jim came alone and often Hannah saw him and Garth out in the field watching and analyzing the horses Garth would be entering along with Raj. *Garth's so busy,* Hannah decided to herself. *Once the race is over, he'll be able to devote more time to his personal life. Besides, when he sees me at the party, I know he'll notice how well I look in my new dress.* She touched the shell around her neck and wished with all her heart for her dreams to come true. And today was the day they might be closer than they ever could be again to coming true.

She had decided to spend the whole day with Garth's horses, making sure everything went perfectly for them; then she would slip away just before the last race so she could spend a little extra time getting ready for the party.

Hannah arrived at the racetrack early, but already the excitement was electrifying the air. The horses could feel it, and they were stamping and snorting impatiently in their stalls. Syces and owners bickered and shouted out orders, and stableboys scurried and scampered between the horses, carrying buckets and saddles and all the assorted gear needed for a horse race. Flags and streamers were all over everything, and people were arriving in their best clothes and most elaborate hats. Even one or two motor cars could be heard chugging around the place.

Hannah scanned the scene looking, as always, for Garth. She was surprised to see him near the stands with a woman on his arm. Her heart sank. For a moment she had the urge to turn and flee. It would be better not to know. But they turned to face her, and Hannah saw the woman was older than Garth. Of course, it was his mother! How could she have forgotten the whole reason for his party? She sighed out loud with relief. Garth caught sight of her and waved.

"Han, old chap, there you are!" Hannah waved shyly back and broke out in her usual furious blush. "Han, this is my mother, Lady Eunice Whitehead. Mother, Hannah Butler, vet." Lady Whitehead nodded politely at Hannah, and Hannah mumbled something about how pleased she was to meet her. She could tell that Garth's mother didn't miss much. She couldn't have missed Hannah's blushing when Garth spoke to her, and Hannah thought she detected her smiling to herself, perhaps with the knowledge that Hannah was in love with her son. But Lady Whitehead had a nice warm smile, and she seemed genuinely interested in the fact that Hannah was a vet.

"Dr. Butler, my son has told me all about you. You have been an invaluable help to him as he has learned about farming this untamed country. I am grateful to you for all you have done for him."

"Oh, I'm sure he would have done just as well without me," Hannah said as she reached to pull her hat down, quite forgetting that she had not brought it. Her hand waved about awkwardly for a minute before she shoved it quickly into her pocket. "Did you have a good trip over?" Hannah asked, glad she had thought of the polite question the visitor is always asked.

"Yes, thank you. The weather held very nicely for us for the entire trip, but we were rather concerned about submarines. There were some very near to us, and there are rumors that we will be blockaded."

"Oh, dear," Hannah replied. The art of starting polite conversations was still so new to her that she hadn't mastered the technique of continuing the conversation. There was an awkward silence for a moment, but Garth spoke up.

"Come, Mother, Han; let's go and look in on the horses."

They went to the stable, where Garth showed his mother his horses and then took her back to her place in the viewing gallery. Hannah stayed in the stables. She felt nervous on Garth's behalf. She could tell that he was anxious to do well in front of his mother. She fingered the amulet and made her usual wishes that Garth would fall in love with her and that his horses would do well.

Raj was Garth's highest hope, and he raced at the end of the day. Hannah was surprised at how quickly the time came. The other two fillies that Garth entered had finished a respectable third and fourth. Hannah supervised as Raj was saddled up and taken out to warm up. She kept waiting for Garth to come and see how his horse was doing, but he only popped down for a moment to make sure that Hannah was there. When he saw she had everything under control, he said he must rush back to be with his mother. Hannah was surprised. Usually he paid much closer attention to his horses.

Hannah watched Raj race from a high point just beside the stables. She hardly dared go any closer because she didn't want her nerves to seep out onto the track and spoil the race for Raj. She could see Garth sitting in a box next to his mother across the field. There didn't seem to be anyone else with them, and Hannah was relieved about that.

Suddenly the gates flew open and the horses thundered out onto the track. She found Raj and was relieved to see he was running beautifully. The jockey hardly had to touch him to make him go, but there was another tall bay horse that was keeping up with him. As the two horses pulled away from the crowd, Raj strained to pull ahead of the bay, but he couldn't get away from him.

They roared around the backstretch, where Hannah could see them closely. The two jockeys were glancing at each other and whipping the horses, but neither could pull away from the other. They came to the last corner. Raj was straining and struggling. The bay began ever so slowly to pull in front of Raj. The jockey was frantic, but nothing he could do could make Raj faster. The bay had more stamina. He had more to give down the final stretch. He didn't even look winded. The race was over. Hannah turned away before Raj crossed the line.

Poor Garth, he was counting on this race so much. Hannah felt so bad for him. He had been convinced that Raj would win and he probably had a lot of money riding on the result. She hung her head and walked slowly back to the stables, where she sat and waited for Raj to be brought in. She wondered if Garth would come too.

When the doors burst open and Raj was brought into his stall, Garth was leading him.

"Han, old chap! Here you are! I've been looking everywhere for you!"

Hannah stared disbelievingly at Garth. He didn't even look concerned about Raj's second-place finish.

"I'm sorry Raj didn't win, Garth. I know it would have meant so much to you if he had." Hannah spoke with as much sympathy as she felt, but Garth just laughed merrily.

"Oh, well, these things will happen. We just didn't count on that beautiful bay, Baron, being as good as he was. But don't worry, we'll get him at the next race, won't we, Raj?" He patted Raj's neck as though Raj was more upset than he was. Hannah didn't know what to say. All the words of condolence that she had been rehearsing seemed suddenly inappropriate.

"Well, you are coming to my party tonight, aren't you, Han? I'm counting on you being there, you know."

"Yes. . .yes, of course," Hannah stammered.

"Good, now, don't be late; I'll be looking out for you!" Garth bent over as he said this and kissed Hannah on the cheek. Before Hannah recovered, he was gone.

She walked over to Raj, who was dejectedly nibbling at some straw on his floor.

"What happened, Raj? Was he just too fast for you? It's alright; you just need a little more training and you'll be beating them all." She stroked Raj's soft nose and he snuffled appreciatively.

"Why doesn't Garth care about it, Raj?" She spoke her thoughts aloud to the horse, "What has gotten into him now? I thought he was going to live or die by the results of this race." Raj just snorted into Hannah's ear.

She gave him a hug and headed off to find Kindye. She had better get home. There was a lot to do before the party tonight if she was going to look her absolute best. Garth's words and kiss came into her mind, and she thrilled at the thought that he was actually looking forward to seeing her tonight. Rosie's magic must be working. She put her hand to her throat to touch the shell and reassure herself.

Sophie was pacing back and forth in her pen when Hannah returned home. She wasn't used to being left at home all day, and clearly she didn't appreciate it. She lifted her trunk and let out an indignant bellow when she saw Hannah.

"Sophie, are you cross with me for leaving you for so long? I'm sorry; I just had to go and help Garth at the track today. Come on, out you come." Hannah opened Sophie's gate and the little elephant trotted out onto the grass. The two of them walked back to the house together. Mrs. Butler was still at the racetrack, and Hannah was grateful for the peace and quiet. But there was someone talking to the servants at the back door when Hannah got there.

"Memsahib!" A young man turned from the door and approached Hannah with a worried look on his face. "I am here with a message from Bwana Osbourne. One of the cows is having difficulty delivering her calf and he wants you to come right away! If you please, memsahib."

Hannah let her shoulders droop visibly and sighed loudly. She wanted to say, "I am busy today," but even as she tried to think of an excuse, she knew that she couldn't just leave the farmer in the lurch with a dead calf and head out to a party where everybody in town would see her.

"Alright, let's go. But I must hurry. I have to get back as quickly as possible." She strode off to the stable to retrieve poor Kindye. Sophie trotted happily along behind her.

"Sophie, you have to stay at home. I'm in too much of a hurry to take you with me, and you'll just be in the way. Kamau!" The syce appeared from the stable. "Saddle Kindye up for me again, will you? I have to help Bwana Osbourne with a difficult delivery. I'll be back as soon as I can, but I need you to take care of Sophie for me or she will follow me. Put her back in her pen."

Within five minutes Hannah was galloping down the

driveway to the clinic to pick up her equipment. She could hear Sophie trumpeting furiously behind her as Kamau restrained her and tried to lead her to her pen. "Rotten cattle," she muttered angrily to herself. "The one day in the entire year when I want to have an evening to myself to go out, they have to have a crisis. I should have known."

She was still in a bad mood when she arrived at the Osbourne farm. Luckily it was not too far from the clinic, and she made good time taking a shortcut across two cow pastures and a coffee field. But the cow was in pain. The calf was breech and there was nothing Jack had been able to do to get it out. Hannah knelt quickly down behind the poor cow and tried her best to deliver the calf with the equipment she had brought along. It seemed to take forever. Hannah was dirty and grimy, not to mention tired, hungry, and very grumpy by the time they got the calf out. It was dead, and the mother was almost dead too. Hannah hurriedly gave Jack instructions for looking after his cow, and jumped up onto Kindye and galloped home.

It was already getting dark and she still had to bathe and wash her hair, not to mention dress and try to put on a little makeup without looking obvious about it. Why, oh why, couldn't she just have had a few minutes to herself to get ready? Garth would be waiting for her tonight. He seemed anxious to see her. If she was ever going to catch him, tonight was the night. Her stomach filled with collywobbles just at the remembrance of Garth's words in the stable this afternoon. "Now or never, Hannah Butler." She said the words out loud as she rushed to the stables.

Kamau came running out to meet her. "Memsahib, memsahib! Sophie ran away. I tried to catch her, but I couldn't keep up. I have sent five totos out to look for her, but she was determined to follow you and I just couldn't keep her back."

Hannah was livid—would nothing go right today? "Well, find her!" she ordered. "I can't help you. I have to go to Bwana Whitehead's now. I don't care how many totos you sent out. You find her. I'm busy tonight and I can't help you."

"But, memsahib!" Kamau protested. "She will not listen to anyone else but you! She won't come unless you call her."

"Well then, she'll have to stay out all night. I am not going to ruin an evening I've been looking forward to for weeks because of a silly animal that won't behave herself. Now, has Memsahib Butler told you to hitch up the buggy?"

"Ndio," Kamau nodded his head and slunk off to the stable. Hannah strode angrily back to the house. Sophie was really turning out to be quite an inconvenience, running off like this on the one night when Hannah couldn't go and find her. Not to mention all the letter writing to Dan to reassure him she was doing fine. Really, how she got herself into this silly arrangement was beyond her. Next time she wrote to Dan she would. . .come to think of it, Hannah suddenly realized it had been several weeks since she had heard from him. A little twinge of worry crossed her mind. She hoped nothing had happened to him. But as quickly as the thought came, she brushed it away; she had other things, very important things, to think about tonight. She would worry about Dan, and for that matter, Sophie, tomorrow. Tonight was her night. She wasn't going to let anything spoil that.

"At last, here you are. Do you realize we are expected at the Whiteheads' in less than an hour!" Mrs. Butler was pacing back and forth impatiently in the lounge. For a moment Hannah had the impression of a ship under full sail. Her mother was swathed from head to toe in pink, her favorite color, from her large, flat hat with the sweeping black ostrich feather and the swirling gauze, to the full chiffon skirt boiling about her ankles as she swept around to face her daughter.

"Don't start, Mother!" Hannah said angrily, and her mother stopped in midturn, stunned for a moment by Hannah's uncharacteristic rudeness.

"Good heavens! How dare you speak to me like that!"

"Mother, I'm in a hurry." Hannah's voice was flat and cold. She strode past her and off to her room.

"Well, I never!" Mrs. Butler commented to the swinging door Hannah had just disappeared through.

The Hannah who reappeared through the door again nearly an hour later was a sight to behold. Her white, strong shoulders rose majestically out of the swath of silk that surrounded her and came together under a beautiful cameo brooch in the center of her bosom. Her hair sparkled like gold where the sun had bleached the topmost curls, and her cheeks were rosy and warm from the sunshine and her own excitement. The bronze silk of her skirt shimmered and gleamed like molten metal as she moved through the room. Even Mrs. Butler was rendered speechless at the sight, and the two of them went out onto the veranda and climbed up onto the waiting buggy.

"Have you found Sophie yet?" Hannah asked, knowing the answer.

"*Hapana,* memsahib," he shook his head and looked worried.

Hannah squelched the flutter of apprehension she felt at the look on his face and flicked the reins. Sophie wasn't stupid. She would find her way home. She would most likely be home before Hannah. *Besides,* Hannah thought as they jogged down the road, *this is my night, my only night, and I intend to make the most of it. I have every right to have one evening of fun in my life and I have no reason to feel guilty about Sophie. If the totos don't find her, she'll surely find her own way back.*

But when Hannah and her mother pulled the buggy up in front of Garth's house, all her bravado shrank and shriveled away to nothing. She looked at all the carriages and horses milling about the driveway. Music rolled out of the open windows and lights poured out into the darkness. Ladies flitted elegantly in and out of the lighted rooms, and the sound of laughter wrapped the whole scene up like silk ribbon. She felt weak with nervousness. Where was Garth? How would she ever find him among all these people? And what if he had forgotten about their conversation that afternoon?

"Well, let's go in; we're late enough as it is." Mrs. Butler's harsh voice jolted Hannah into action. She threw the reins down to a waiting syce and stepped carefully down from the buggy. Then she reached up to hand her mother down. The two of them ascended the veranda steps and hesitated. Even Mrs. Butler suddenly seemed daunted by the scene before her. Hannah felt panic rising in her breast, but just as she thought she would have to slip away and pretend she never came, Garth's familiar "Han, old chap!" reached out and stopped her.

Garth himself stepped out onto the veranda to greet them, but the second he saw Hannah he stopped dead in his tracks. Hannah felt his eyes take in her dress and her shoulders, her neck and her cheeks, and finally reach her eyes. They looked at each other for a long moment, and Hannah saw admiration and pleasure in his look. This was new to her. No one had ever looked at her that way, except perhaps Dan, but then that didn't really count. As she smiled at Garth, the thought of Dan brought that flicker of worry to her mind for a moment, but it was too distant a thing compared to the reality of Garth smiling like this at her and offering her his arm to escort her inside.

She took a deep breath and slipped her arm through his.

Neither she nor Garth even remembered Mrs. Butler, who followed them inside, but it didn't matter because Mrs. Butler was glad enough that it was her daughter who was going into the party like Cinderella with her prince. Like magic, the music started up just as they entered the door, and Garth turned to Hannah.

"May I have this dance, Miss Butler?"

Hannah couldn't speak. Even she hadn't dared to imagine that the evening would start off like this. But Garth didn't bother with her answer. Before she could gather herself together, he had gathered her into his arms and they were waltzing around and around the dance floor.

"You look exquisite tonight," Garth was breathing the words into her ear. Hannah felt herself blush with pleasure right from the top of her head down to her bare shoulders. "Thank you." She could barely bring herself to speak. The sound of her own everyday voice might break this breathtaking spell. The last thing she had done before she left her room that evening was to sew Rosie's shell into the bodice of her dress. She could feel it now, pressing into her soft flesh just above her heart. It surely was magic.

"I'm so glad you came." There was the whisper again. "I was worried when you were late."

Luckily, just as Hannah was trying to bring herself to reply, the music died away and the swirling couples drifted away. Garth drew Hannah to him in an imperceptible hug before he let her go.

"Come," he said, looking warmly down at her, "I'd like you to meet my mother."

"I met her this afternoon at the races. Remember?"

"Oh, yes, of course. Well, she mentioned what a nice and interesting person you are, so I thought I'd take you to see her again, if you don't mind."

"No, of course I'd love to see her."

Lady Whitehead was sitting on a couch speaking to a cluster of women scattered about her on assorted chairs.

"Mother!" said Garth, marching boldly into their midst. "Do you remember Hannah Butler? You met this afternoon at the track."

"Oh, yes, of course I remember. It is my pleasure, Miss Butler. Do sit down and join us. Garth, fetch the young lady some punch. You would like some punch, wouldn't you, Miss Butler?"

Hannah nodded and sat down on the chair Garth had drawn up for her. Lady Whitehead was dressed in black, but she had a soft, blue wool shawl drawn cozily about her, giving her a warm and gentle appearance. *Almost fragile,* Hannah thought. But there was a sense of determination about her, especially in her eyes. Hannah remembered that from this morning. No wonder Garth paid so much attention to her opinions.

Garth returned promptly with a glass of punch for Hannah, but he didn't stay. Hannah was left with the panicky thought that she was expected to entertain Lady Whitehead. But her fears were groundless because Lady Whitehead was a very gracious and skilled conversationalist. She put Hannah at ease quickly and easily by admiring her chosen profession and stating that if she had her way, women would be allowed much more freedom in choosing their own life's work. Then she asked Hannah all about her work, her life as a child in Africa, and how she liked it here now.

Hannah found herself chatting easily and without shyness with Lady Whitehead. Out of the corner of her eye, she caught Garth watching her sometimes, but there were also a few times she noticed him dancing with several of the more glamorous young women.

Hannah stayed with Lady Whitehead until dinner was

served. Garth came over to escort his mother into the dining room and to Hannah's surprise and consternation, he offered her his other arm. Hannah took it shyly, and immediately she felt the glares of several of the other ladies boring into her bare back. It was an uncomfortable sensation, but she was also quite gratified to see the surprised look on her mother's face as she swept past her on Garth's arm with Lady White-head on the other side.

Garth seated himself next to Hannah at dinner. She was grateful to him for refraining from referring to her as "old chap" all evening. But even as she watched him chat with and smile at the other guests, she couldn't help wondering why Raj's second-place finish that afternoon didn't seem to have affected his mood at all.

She noticed Jim and Fiona sitting further down the table. They were too far away to speak to, although Fiona smiled grimly at Hannah when she saw her seated next to Garth. Jim looked particularly miserable. He hardly made any effort to speak to the other people around him, and Hannah even thought she saw Fiona nudge him sharply to make him pay attention to something someone was telling him. *Fiona is laughing awfully loudly and shrilly,* Hannah thought. But she didn't have a chance to watch them any more because Garth was speaking to her. Every time he said anything to her, it was as though they were the only two people at the table.

"Do you like my mother?" he asked her quietly when the others around them were involved in a loud discussion about how long they felt the war would last.

"Yes, of course. She is a very nice person. I enjoyed speaking to her very much." Hannah was surprised that he cared about her opinion of his mother.

A few minutes later he leaned toward her and asked, "Do

you think this pheasant is properly cooked? I told my cook that it had to be well done, but I have so much trouble with the help, as you know from what happened to King. Still, I wouldn't want anyone to become ill."

Hannah stopped chewing. With all the excitement, she had hardly noticed what she was eating, but she nodded quickly. "Yes, it is very nicely cooked."

When the creme caramel was served later in the evening, Garth leaned over again. "You dance very well. I would be honored if you would save a few dances for me after the meal."

Hannah looked at him in surprise. Then she looked shyly down at her plate and said, "I'm sure I won't be booked at all. It would be very nice to dance with you."

"Well, I wouldn't count on your being free. You do look very lovely tonight, and I think there are quite a few young men who have noticed that fact."

Hannah didn't know what to say in response to this. Finally she blurted out the question on her mind all evening. "Garth, aren't you feeling badly about Raj not winning the race this afternoon? I know you were counting so much on him winning."

Garth laughed. *A little hollow,* Hannah thought. "Well, I would have liked him to win, that's true, but there is only so much one can do to make it happen. Still, he's a good little horse, and I'm sure there will be many other chances for him to win. And if you keep helping me the way you have been, I know we can make a winning team." Again, Hannah didn't know how to respond. This evening was turning out to be altogether unpredictable.

"I think we do very well together. We can only get better, don't you agree, Hannah?" Hannah looked up at Garth in dismay. How could she answer questions like this? What was he getting at? But Garth was looking at her with a very serious, intense look in his eyes. Again Hannah felt as though there were only the two of them at the table. She nodded her agreement, and Garth's face relaxed into a smile.

When dinner was finished and all the guests were slowly filtering back into the lounge, Garth took Hannah by the hand and led her onto the dance floor. As they whirled around and around, Hannah found the time to wonder why this was so easy. If she had known how easy it was to have Garth White-head pay attention to her, she should have tried it ages ago. But she had the distinct feeling that she was missing something here. The evening was not hers to seize the way she had planned; it was Garth's. It was under his control. She felt the shell pressing into her breast. Perhaps that was it. It was neither her nor Garth, but Rosie's magic. However, as she thought about it, now that she was living in the reality of dancing with Garth, floating and flying around the room in his arms, the magic shell was really just a silly, insignificant thing compared to reality. She wished for a moment that she could slip it out of her dress and throw it away.

The music was dying and Garth took her elbow and steered her to where the band was stationed. He whispered something into the leader's ear and in a few minutes the music started again. This time the music was slow and romantic. Hannah felt her breath taken away as Garth took her into his arms again, pulled her close, and lay his cheek next to hers. She hardly dared breathe. Her heart was beating so hard, he must feel it. But he said nothing. Not until the end of the dance.

"Come, Hannah, let's walk in the garden." He took her by the hand and led her out onto the veranda.

Hannah was overwhelmed. She could only register sensations in her mind. She felt the strength and control in Garth's hand over hers, and the sensation of smiling and nodding at other guests as she wove through them behind Garth. When they stepped out onto the veranda, she felt the music and chatter die away behind her as the door closed. She stepped into a dark, cool world of sweet perfume mingled with the faint smokiness of distant fires. The buzzing, chirping, and gentle cooing of the evening insects and birds wrapped around her. As Garth took her in his arms, his nearness and the familiar musky scent of his cologne blotted out everything else around her.

In a minute he drew away from her, and she felt his hand reach for her face and lift it up to his own. Then the touch of his lips on hers sent a thrill of joy throughout her body, and there was nothing else left in Hannah's world except that feeling for a long time. Later, he drew away. Hannah could feel the cool, quiet African night envelope her again, and she saw a blanket of stars swirling above Garth's head. Garth was speaking to her, but his words were only sounds, the tone husky and the feeling pure joy. Her mind didn't take them in. She smiled back and he bent to kiss her again. And after he kissed her, she heard his words at last.

"Hannah, will you marry me? We've known each other a long time and we would make a good team, don't you think?"

Hannah was startled. She stepped backwards and turned away from him, his kiss still imprinted on her lips and his words swirling through her mind. She felt his hands on her shoulders and his voice sounded in her ear.

"Please marry me, Hannah. You and I belong together." His voice had a coaxing note to it, the way he would speak to a balky colt. As he spoke the words, all the romance of the evening fell away, and Hannah's mind kicked into motion. This was the moment she had been dreaming of all these months. It was actually here. Yet the idea of actually making the dream into a reality suddenly, without warning, transformed it into a nightmare—all the people who would have to be told, what they would say, her life with Garth, parties, races, new dresses, and teas. What would happen to her life? Would he love her alone? The thought sliced like a cold knife into her mind. Inexplicably, Dan's face appeared and she wished she could talk to him.

But Garth was twisting her around to face him and again he kissed her, hard and demandingly, making her feel powerless. When he was finished, she said, "Yes, I will."

eight

Hannah woke early the following morning after only a few hours of sleep. She lay still for a moment trying to remember what had happened the night before that gave her a feeling of dread. And then it broke through her mind like a flash flood, roaring down the dry but peaceful stream that her life had been so far and uprooting everything in its path. She had actually agreed to marry Garth, she remembered, but it hadn't quite turned out the way she dreamed it would. At first it was nice, when only the two of them knew and he was kissing her and holding her in his arms. But then, they had gone inside and he had announced that he had to say something. He had stood up on the platform where the band was playing and pulled her up there after him. Hannah had cringed with embarrassment at the stunned looks on the faces of all his guests. She had tried to smile bravely back into their faces, but she had wanted to run. This wasn't at all what it was supposed to feel like.

"Friends," Garth had begun, pulling Hannah towards him and putting his arm around her waist. There was a shocked silence and Hannah had continued to smile bravely into it. "Friends, this is the happiest day of my life. Hannah Butler— I think you all know Hannah—has done me the great honor of agreeing to marry me." Hannah felt rather than heard the guests gasp, but someone had begun to clap. It was her mother. Gradually the rest of the group took the cue and clapped too. Garth held up his hand. "Thank you, thank you. I had a case of champagne saved in the icebox just in case I would have the pleasure of celebrating my engagement. . . our engagement here tonight. I hardly dared to hope, and yet my prayers have been answered. Please join me in a toast, everyone." He jumped down to the floor and handed Hannah down after him. Instantly Hannah had been surrounded by a throng of guests. Some shook her by the hand, but most of them kissed her politely on the cheek and offered their best wishes.

"Well, well, this is a surprise. Who would have thought our Garth would ever settle down. All the best to you, my dear."

"My, aren't you the sly one, stealing Garth right out from under our noses. But I do wish you both much happiness."

"My word, you certainly took us all by surprise, Hannah Butler. Who would have thought you of all people. . . But let me congratulate you both."

"So, how long have you been keeping this little secret? You certainly had everyone completely baffled!"

"What a shock, I mean, surprise. . ."

"I had no idea. . ."

"When did this all happen?"

And on it went. Hannah's smile was plastered to her face, but it was getting very tattered and tired, she remembered, before everyone finally began to drift home. She had begun to think the night would go on forever. Garth flitted around making sure the champagne kept flowing and stopped beside Hannah now and then to accept someone or another's heartfelt congratulations.

As she lay there in the morning watching her curtains twitch with the early morning breeze, Hannah recalled that only Lady Whitehead hadn't seemed very surprised. She hadn't seemed very pleased, either, come to think of it. She started out well, but. . .

"Hannah, my dear, I can't imagine a nicer girl than you marrying my son."

"Thank you, Lady Whitehead," Hannah had replied, looking up just in time to see Garth smiling approvingly across the room at them.

"Garth never told me you and he were romantically involved."

"Yes, I know; it is a bit sudden." Hannah felt herself blushing. "But we have known each other a long time, Lady Whitehead. We work together very closely with Garth's horses."

"Ah, I see. You love him, then?"

"Yes. . .yes, of course."

"Well, my dear, I hate to be less than thrilled for you and Garth, but please understand; I think you are a fine girl. It is just my son's motives that I worry about."

"Lady Whitehead. . .are you trying to tell me he doesn't love me?" Hannah had felt anger rising. How dare this lady who had only been in the country for a few days tell her how her son felt about her!

Lady Whitehead had taken Hannah's hands in her own. "No, no, my dear. I didn't mean to upset you. It is only because I really do like you, even though we've only just met. It is Garth I am worried about. He can be so fickle sometimes, you know, and I don't want anything to be amiss. Just promise me you won't let him rush you into this. Take your time and make sure that he loves you as much as you deserve."

"I'm sure he does, Lady Whitehead."

"That's good, my dear. But, nevertheless, don't rush into it." With that, she had bent and kissed Hannah on the cheek. Garth had come over and put his arm around Hannah again, which she had been grateful for.

Looking back on that conversation, Hannah still couldn't make much sense of it. She would have understood if Lady Whitehead had been angry with Garth for marrying some-one beneath him. After all, that would have been true. But to suggest that Garth didn't really love her? Now that she thought about it in the clear and harsh light of the morning, the idea gave her a very strange, sickly sensation in the pit of her stomach. She wished she could just ride over to his house right now and ask him about it. It was always a com-fort to know that no matter how badly she felt about Garth when she was not with him, he had the knack of banishing all those thoughts just by his mere presence with her. Soon she would be with him forever and the worrying thoughts would be gone. Forever.

As she lay there thinking, Hannah heard Kerioki bringing the morning tea. First he took a tray to her mother's room; a few minutes later, she heard the door close and a soft knock on her own door.

"Come in, Kerioki," Hannah said, sitting up.

Kerioki came in and put the tray down on the bedside table.

"Memsahib, I have a message from Rosie for you this morning."

"Yes, what is it?"

"Memsahib, Rosie wants to come to see you this morning."

"Thank you, Kerioki. Tell Rosie to come to me after break-fast. And tell her not to worry; I know what I am doing." Hannah was fairly certain Rosie must have heard the news.

"*Ndio,* 'sahib," Kerioki nodded and slipped out the door.

Hannah sipped her tea thoughtfully. The strange fear in the pit of her stomach had returned. *But that's just because of Rosie's message,* she thought. It was so frustrating to be tossed about by every whim of her feelings. But of course that would all change once she and Garth were actually married.

After they were married, would Garth expect her to give up her practice? She knew he would still want to give the parties and they would spend a lot of time at the club. Of course when he was married, he would have a wife and perhaps soon there would be children, reasons enough to stay at home. She hoped her company would be reason enough for Garth. She sighed. Why were there so many undercurrents in her thoughts this morning? After all, surely it was the happiest morning of her life, and she wasn't happy enough. There must be something wrong with her.

She looked out of her window, between her blowing curtains. And then it dawned on her. Sophie! Where was Sophie? Usually she waited for Hannah on the lawn in the mornings. She must have come back last night. Maybe she was just tired out from all her adventures and was not eating her breakfast as quickly as usual. Hannah jumped up and threw her dressing gown around her shoulders.

"Kerioki! Kerioki!" She rushed down the hall to the kitchen and burst through the door. Kerioki and the cook and a toto were sitting at the kitchen table while sausages and bacon sizzled gently on the stove behind them. They looked up in surprise when they saw Hannah, but they did not smile. Hannah hardly noticed.

"Kerioki, where's Sophie? She came back last night, didn't she?"

Kerioki stood up, looking confused and unhappy. "I–I don't know, memsahib. Perhaps the syce would know. You must ask him, I think."

Hannah looked at the cook and the toto. They were both staring at her with inscrutable expressions on their faces. Hannah whirled around and stormed out of the door. Striding down the hall to return to her room and get dressed, she almost bumped into her mother just coming out of her own room.

"Hannah, what are you doing up so early? You had such a night last night, you should be getting some beauty sleep. You can just tell those farmers at that clinic of yours that they will have to wait. You have a wedding to plan! There is so much to do! Oh, my goodness, I can't believe this is happening to us!"

Mrs. Butler's face was flushed with excitement and she obviously hadn't slept much either. She took Hannah by the elbow and steered her to her room.

"You simply must go back to bed, my dear. I will take care of everything. You get your rest. You want to look your best for your fiancé and if I do say so, you look like an absolute fright this morning!"

"Mother!" Hannah turned to face her when they got to her room. "Do you know where Sophie is? I haven't seen her this morning. I must go out to the stables and check that she is alright."

"Oh, for heaven's sake, Hannah Butler! You have other matters to consider now. You are engaged to Garth White-head! Don't worry about that creature. You shouldn't have said you would take her on. Now you are going to have to get rid of her. You cannot possibly take her to the Whiteheads' with you, and I cannot have her here with me. You'll just have to write and tell Mr. Williams that due to unforeseen circumstances, you cannot keep her for him. He will have to make other arrangements.

"Now, come along, there is a lot to do, but first you must get rested in case Garth calls on us today. It simply would not do to have him regretting what he has done if he sees you looking like this. Now, off you go. I'll send Kerioki in with some breakfast later."

Suddenly there was a commotion outside and the sound of footsteps on the veranda. "Oh, no! He's here already! Get dressed at once!" Mrs. Butler shrieked as she shoved Hannah into her bedroom and slammed the door behind her.

Hannah heard a sharp rap on the door as she threw on her usual trousers and white blouse. What was he doing here so early? Could he have regretted last night and come to call it off? The thoughts panicked Hannah as she tried to slap some water on her face and drag her brush through her hair. She could hear her mother's footsteps coming down the hall. She fought off the impulse to climb out of her window and run away. How would she face the town if he called the engagement off? The humiliation would be unbearable. She must run. The door burst open and Mrs. Butler stood there, looking angry.

"Jack Osbourne is here to see you. If he wants you to go over to his place at this hour of the morning, you just tell him you can't. You are engaged now, Hannah, and you have far more urgent duties to consider than someone's sick cattle!"

Hannah sighed with relief. So it wasn't Garth. "It's alright, Mother. I am still the vet." She strode confidently down the hall.

Jack was standing in the lounge holding his hat in both his hands, twisting it around and around. He looked about as comfortable as a zebra in a lion's den.

"Jack! What can I do for you this morning?" Hannah put her hand out to shake his.

He didn't answer her question. "Miss Butler, I have very bad news for you. I am terribly sorry, but I shot your pet elephant last night. A herd had gone through my maize two nights ago, and I thought they had come back to finish it off. I saw the elephant standing in the field, eating, and I assumed that where you see one elephant, there are more. So

I shot it, just to warn the others off, you know. But there were no others and when I went out there this morning, I realized it was the little elephant you are boarding for that missionary chap who went off to war. I'm terribly sorry, Miss Butler. If there's anything I can do to make amends. . ."

Hannah stared at him in disbelief. His voice trailed off as he looked into her face and the two of them stood silently for a moment.

"I'm awfully sorry. It was an accident," Jack stammered, looking as if he would take off with fright at any moment.

At that moment, Mrs. Butler bustled importantly into the room. "Hannah, have you told Mr. Osbourne your wonderful news? Jim, if you haven't heard already, congratulations are in order for my daughter. She became engaged last night! To Mr. Garth Whitehead! I'm sure she won't be keeping up her veterinary practice now that she is engaged, will you, Hannah, my dear?"

Jack stepped hesitantly forward and shook Hannah's hand again. "Congratulations, Miss Butler. And again, I'm awfully sorry." Then he turned and fled.

Mrs. Butler stared at the door, then turned to Hannah. "What on earth was that all about? What does he mean that he's sorry? Sorry!"

Hannah sank into the nearest chair and put her head into her hands and began to cry.

"Well, I never!" said her mother angrily. "What an unbelievably rude man! That is what you get for associating with the lower classes, who have absolutely no manners whatsoever! But at least we can take comfort in knowing it won't last much longer. Soon you'll be keeping a far better class of company. And not a moment too soon, I say!

"Come now, Hannah, there's no need to be so upset about it. You are just a little overwrought with all the excitement, and everything happening so suddenly. You just lie down in your room for a few minutes." She tried to urge Hannah out of her chair by taking her by the elbow, but Hannah shook her off.

"Mother! He came to tell me that he accidentally shot Sophie last night. Sophie is dead, Mother. What will I do now? And how will I tell Dan?" She burst into a renewed bout of sobbing.

Mrs. Butler stood looking at her daughter with confusion. "Well, my dear, it is rather a tragedy," she began when Hannah had calmed down slightly, "but wasn't I just telling you a few minutes ago that you would have to get rid of the creature anyway, now that you're engaged? So it is for the best. You'll get over it. You have much bigger fish to fry now. Come along, my dear, pull yourself together and go and lie down. I wouldn't wonder if your fiancé didn't come over to see you this morning. I know what young men who are in love are like. They have absolutely no idea what an engagement entails if you are a woman. But he mustn't see you looking like this."

Hannah looked up incredulously at her mother and caught sight of Rosie standing behind her in the doorway. She could tell by the stricken look on Rosie's face that she had been there long enough to have heard what happened to Sophie.

"Oh, Rosie, thank goodness you're here!" Hannah stood up and went over to her. "What am I going to do, Rosie? Sophie's dead. What will I tell Dan?"

Rosie steered Hannah toward her bedroom. "Your mother is right, Miss Hannah; you must come with me and lie down." She led Hannah to her room as though she were still a little girl. It felt good to feel her strong arms guiding her down the hall. Rosie tucked her back into her bed and drew the curtains shut.

"We'll talk this afternoon. You rest now. You are very tired."

Hannah lay in the filtered daylight. How would she explain to Dan that she had left Sophie and gone off to a party at Garth's without even bothering to make sure Sophie was home safely? It would only have taken her a few minutes to have made sure Sophie was secure in her boma. After all, she should have known that Sophie would try to follow her. And now, because of her own selfish carelessness, Sophie was dead. Automatically, she reached for the shell around her neck. She had put it back on the leather thong when she took off her dress last night. As she touched the warm, smooth shell, the whole idea of magic, of making Garth fall in love with her against his own natural desires, seemed repulsive beyond belief. What if there were such a thing as magic? What if it had actually worked for her and that was the only reason Garth was marrying her? What if it was an evil thing? Dan would say it was evil. At the very least it was profoundly selfish and manipulative, the opposite of what Dan said God was. He said God was unselfish, loving, and giving. A feeling of repulsion and loathing for the thing around her neck rose in Hannah's throat and she yanked so hard on it that it broke off. She could feel a stinging welt around her neck as the leather broke against her skin, but she felt relief to be rid of it. She got out of bed, pulled open her curtain, and hurled the thing away, not even waiting to see where it landed. Then slowly she crawled back into her bed and prayed.

"Oh God, please forgive me. Please let Dan forgive me, too, God. I'm so sorry." Hannah said the words aloud into her pillow. Over and over again she repeated them and gradually her shock subsided and she began to think.

She found herself thinking of Dan and how he prayed. She

remembered how sure he seemed that God loved him and how he said that God loved her too. If God had loved her, surely He wouldn't any longer, not after what she had done.

But then who is forgiveness for if not for people that you love? She wished she knew more about forgiveness. She wished she had thought more about the old Sunday school stories about Jesus dying on the cross.

"Oh, Jesus, please, please forgive me for this. And make Dan forgive me too," she prayed aloud again.

❧

She felt better when she awoke a few hours later. She heard lunch being carried out onto the veranda, and she realized she was hungry. Then she remembered Sophie. Sorrow and guilt overwhelmed her. She heard footsteps coming down the hall. Her stomach knotted as her door opened quietly.

"Oh, good, you're awake." It was her mother. "Lunch is ready. And Garth sent over a message to invite us both for tea this afternoon. He said his mother was looking forward to getting to know us better.

"Just think; I haven't a decent thing to wear and neither have you, but there's not a thing we can do about it until we can get up to Nairobi to do some shopping. Oh, Hannah, you should have warned me that you were thinking of becoming engaged and we could have been prepared. This is such an embarrassment—actually to be invited to tea with Lady Whitehead and on such dreadfully short notice!"

"I'll be there in a minute, Mother," Hannah said, wearily getting out of bed. Her hunger had vanished. Tea with Lady Whitehead and her mother and Garth. It didn't bear thinking about. As she tried to push the thought out of her mind, she had a vision of her whole future: an endless round of tea parties, cocktail parties, dinner parties, and dances whirl-pooling off into the distance, sucking her deeper and deeper until she died. She shook her head to free herself from the horrible thought. "It must be because I feel so awful about losing Sophie that I have become so morbid. I am actually engaged to be married to Garth Whitehead. This is the happiest day of my life. I must remember that." And with that thought held resolutely before her, Hannah marched out to the veranda.

However, eating turned out to be an entirely different matter. The cold roast beef and the jellied braun set out at the table turned her stomach. And there was a letter on the table waiting for her. It bore an English stamp, not a European one, and for a moment Hannah dared to hope it wasn't from Dan. But she recognized his handwriting on the envelope.

"There, now you can write back to that young man and apologize for losing his elephant and at the same time mention that you are engaged to Mr. Whitehead. It will be good to have done with him. I didn't really like him at all, the way he trailed around after you whenever he had a chance. I was almost beginning to think he was in love with you. But you write to him directly and explain."

Hannah tore open the envelope with trembling hands and began to read.

Dear Hannah,

I am writing to you from a hospital in England. I took a shell to the legs and seem to be full of shrapnel. My left leg can be repaired quite easily with a bit of minor surgery, but it is still touch and go for my right leg. I am thankful to God, because I am one of the lucky ones who escaped the shelling with my life. But it looks as though I will be out of commission and will have to be sent home. I miss Africa terribly, as you know, as well as Sophie, and of course, you too. I hope to come out on

*the very first ship as soon as I am well enough to travel.
Please pray that the Lord will be gracious enough to
save my leg for me so that I may be able to continue my
work. And give my love to Sophie. I am so grateful to
you for taking care of her for me. God willing, I'll be
home soon.*

In Christ's love,
Dan

Silently, Hannah put the letter back into the envelope, but Mrs. Butler had recognized the handwriting.

"Well, how is your Mr. Williams?" Mrs. Butler began as soon as she saw Hannah was finished reading the letter. But she didn't wait for Hannah's answer. "You and Garth could well be married by the time the war is over! Of course, we must set the date right away. I'm sure all the Whitehead family in England need to be notified and given enough time to attend, if they should choose to. And then there are our own relations. . ."

Hannah wasn't listening. She pushed her chair out from the table and put on her old hat.

"Hannah, come back! You haven't touched your lunch!" But Hannah just kept walking. She wanted to go over to the Osbourne place and arrange to bury Sophie.

nine

The days after her engagement turned out just as Hannah had feared. She hardly had time for her practice at all with all the shopping and partying. Everyone assumed she would be giving it up anyway after she was married, and she didn't have the courage yet to tell them that she didn't plan to. But the wedding, much to Mrs. Butler's consternation, was not going to be imminent. Lady Whitehead had had them over to tea on the first day, the day Sophie had died, and suggested again to Hannah and her mother that a long engagement would be a good idea. It would give Hannah time to think through her decision, she said, and then there was also the problem of the war. Garth had agreed, saying that he didn't want to rush Hannah into anything. He had wanted her to take all the time she needed to be sure.

"But, she is sure!" Mrs. Butler had protested. "Aren't you Hannah, dear?"

But Hannah had smiled gratefully up at Garth, and Lady Whitehead had inquired whether Mrs. Butler had seen the gardens. She had not and so the two of them went for a tour, leaving Hannah and Garth together on the patio.

In Garth's shining presence, all the qualms Hannah had felt about marrying him dried up to nothing, and she basked in the pleasure of his attention.

"Well, Han, old chap," he said smiling at her as he reached over to take her hand in his, "this is quite a situation we've gotten ourselves into, isn't it?" Then he bent over the table and kissed her. "I.hope you aren't having second thoughts."

"Oh, no, of course not!" Hannah replied, only remembering the happiness she felt when they were together. He kissed her again.

"I've been thinking, Hannah," he spoke again. The suddenly serious tone in his voice sent a fearful shiver down Hannah's spine. "Jim and I have been talking about a safari company for quite a while, and I think I will go along with his idea. There is a lot of money to be made off people who want to be taken out on safari to bag some big game. Trophy hunters generally can afford to pay a pretty price to get what they want." Hannah looked silently up into his blue eyes. She knew what was coming next, but she didn't want to hurry it, so she waited.

"So you see, Han, old chap, it would be a bit awkward having a new wife and to be off on safari all the time. I was just thinking that perhaps we could prolong our engagement for a little while longer than I first thought, just until Jim and I get the business up and running. Then, of course, I wouldn't need to be out on safari all the time. Jim and I could alternate and we could both spend more time at home with our wives."

NO! NO! NO! Hannah's mind screamed. *He is putting me off. I must fight for him.* She had come so close; she couldn't let him go now. She forced herself to think. What could she say? Jim was the answer.

"But what about Jim? What will Jim do with his farm if he is on safari all the time? And Fiona? What will Fiona do?" She knew she was speaking too fast and her voice sounded high-pitched and desperate. Garth smiled. She could see he already had thought that through.

"Hannah, Hannah, you sound so upset. Don't worry, my dearest, it is only temporary." Hannah could feel her face turning red with rage at the patronizing tone of his voice, but his next words made her forget her anger.

"And really, I am doing it all to help Jim and Fiona out. Didn't you know that they have lost their farm? It seems that Jim had lost quite a bit of money on the horse races this season and he had to put his farm up for sale to pay the debts off. They are moving into town, so Jim will need to find some other work. This will be the perfect opportunity for him to support Fiona and rebuild his life. I really am doing it as a favor for him. It is important to make absolutely sure the business is a complete success, for his sake. And Fiona's too."

Hannah was speechless. She had had no idea that Fiona and Jim were in such trouble. She thought back to the day Fiona had asked her to pray for her and how she had prayed once and then never given it another thought. The rest of what Garth said washed over her like a rainstorm. She just trudged on through it until Garth kissed her good-bye and she and her mother drove home.

She hadn't even really spoken to Fiona for such a long time. She wondered if she could do anything to make amends for how much she had neglected the only real friend she had ever had.

Mrs. Butler chatted gaily on about the wonders of Garth's home and the charms of his mother as they bumped over the red, dusty roads. Hannah could see a storm building on the horizon, but she thought if she urged Kindye into a trot, they would be home in time.

She couldn't stop thinking about Fiona. It was the first time in weeks that she had really been able to think of anyone but Garth, only this time she felt very guilty and ashamed. Would Fiona be able to forgive her if she went and spoke to her and apologized for having been so self-centered?

By the time they reached home, just as the first furious drops of rain were lashing the treetops, she had made up her mind that she must at least visit Fiona and apologize. If Fiona were able to forgive her, then she would try to think of how she could help her. But Fiona was in the midst of moving, according to Garth. She would have to wait a week or two until she had settled into her new home. This would give Hannah time to think through how she would approach Fiona.

In the days that followed, Hannah lived for the moments when she and Garth were alone together and he was touching her and looking into her eyes and reassuring her that everything was going to be wonderful after they were married, but they must wait. But in between those moments there were the parties and the shopping and the teas, and these in turn had to be fitted around Hannah's practice delivering calves, repairing wounds, and caring for sick horses. Hannah wondered if she saw less of Garth now than she did before they had become engaged. He never asked her to go to the stables and look at his horses anymore. In fact, he didn't seem to have the same degree of interest that he used to have in racing. These days, all he seemed to talk about with his friends was safaris and big-game hunting. That was where all the money was to be made, they all said. He and Jim were planning a big safari soon, as soon as they felt safe enough to travel. And once the war was over, they would start a safari company and make lots of money. And of course, the war would surely be over soon. *But the news from Europe is not very encouraging,* Hannah thought.

Hannah found herself thinking of Sophie every time they spoke of safaris. She hated to think of Garth, her own husband, stalking and shooting elephants. Every time they shot an elephant, she would remember Sophie being shot. She knew this was a silly thing, but she was finding it hard to get over Sophie's death. It had taken her two weeks to get up the courage to write to Dan and confess to letting her run away and be killed. But she felt better when she had done it because she hadn't tried to hide her own role in Sophie's death. She had asked Dan to forgive her, but she couldn't bring herself to tell him about her engagement. She would tell him in person, she decided, when he finally came back, and that might not be for a long time. Meanwhile, she missed the little elephant trotting around after her wherever she went.

At the interminable dinner parties that she now went to with Garth, she often found herself wishing she were out in the stables settling Sophie in for the evening. She tried to behave with grace and good humor, but Garth's friends really had very little in common with her. At first they were very condescending, saying things like, "Well, Miss Butler. You are a vet, I believe. How nice. Garth must have relied on you to help him a lot with his horses."

Or, "I suppose being so 'horsey' as you are, you and Garth must have quite a lot to talk about. Isn't that so romantic?"

Or, "My dear, we were all so shocked to hear that Garth had finally become engaged. How on earth did you manage to snare him? You must have a secret weapon." The ladies would exchange knowing looks across the table at each other, and Hannah wouldn't know how to reply. She counted the hours until Garth would drive her home in his buggy.

One evening when she and Garth were at the Kikuru Club and Garth had rushed off to talk to some gentlemen, she was looking over the ladies present to see whom she could approach when she noticed Leticia. Her heart sank. Leticia had been in South Africa visiting relatives, so she hadn't seen her since before her engagement. Just as she was about to duck quickly behind a potted palm, Leticia caught her eye. Hannah winced and braced herself as Leticia made her way over to her, looking grimly cheerful in a beautiful cream silk dress that had far too many little fashionable touches in the cut of the sleeves and the scoop of the neckline ever to have been bought in Nairobi.

"Congratulations, Miss Butler. I hear you and Garth are engaged." Leticia's voice had a very slight edge of anger to it, Hannah thought, but then none of Garth's lady friends had been exactly overjoyed at his engagement.

"Yes," Hannah replied, "we've been engaged for nearly a month now."

"Oh, really? I have just arrived from South Africa, where I was visiting my mother, so I only just heard. I must say I was quite surprised. I thought you looked after his horses." Leticia spoke to Hannah as though she were an upstart of a servant, marrying her master. This was by far the rudest treatment she had received yet, and she blushed with anger and embarrassment.

"Hannah, I was hoping to find you here tonight!" Hannah turned to see who was speaking. To her relief she looked into the warm face of Fiona Brown.

"Oh, Fiona," she gasped, "I'm so sorry. I heard about—" Suddenly she remembered that Leticia was there and probably didn't know Fiona's situation. She stopped.

Fiona took Hannah by the elbow and looked at Leticia. "Excuse me, Miss Charlesworth, but I must just borrow Miss Butler for a moment," and she steered Hannah away. Hannah silently complied, not knowing what to make of Fiona's new friendliness.

"Hannah," she said when they were alone, "I feel awful about my behavior towards you lately. Please forgive me for being so rude and unfriendly. I must apologize to you. I have been unforgivably rude to you since you and Garth became engaged and it was completely uncalled for. I was angry with Garth because I thought he was the one who was leading my husband astray and making him spend all our money on the horse races. And I lumped you in with my feelings about Garth. I hope you'll forgive me."

Hannah blushed to the roots of her hair. "Oh, Fiona, don't mention it, please; it is I who has behaved rudely toward you. I had no idea you and Jim were encountering such difficulties, and I haven't been a friend to you at all. I have only been thinking of myself. I am so sorry, Fiona."

Impulsively, Fiona reached forward and hugged her. "You must come and see me in my new home, Hannah," she said as they walked over to sit together and talk.

Hannah hardly noticed the evening fly by, even though she hadn't seen much of Garth. And then he sent her home with his syce, rather than driving her home himself. He kissed her good-bye as he handed her up into the buggy, and she was bouncing along the road in the moonlight without Garth.

Secretly she felt grateful for the reprieve. She was getting very weary, with work during the day and being out late two or three nights a week. And there was so much to worry about all the time, as her mother made clear. She must buy clothes and shoes and all sorts of bits and pieces to complement them. Mrs. Butler dragged her up to Nairobi several times for shopping sprees. These days were exhausting and long, although Hannah did enjoy the new clothes. She surprised herself with this discovery. She had never been interested in clothes before, but now she began to like the looks of herself in beautiful colors and fabrics. She had to admit she also liked the effect her new appearance had on Garth and the other men in his circle. This was a new feeling for Hannah.

But during the next few weeks, when Hannah seemed slightly tired, Garth often sent her home before him with the syce. She would try to insist that she was having a lovely time and would wait for him, but he wouldn't hear of it. She looked peaked, he would say, or something similar, as he walked her out to the waiting buggy and kissed her goodnight. Hannah thought the ordeal of the dinner parties wasn't really worth it for a quick peck on the cheek at the end of the evening.

One morning Hannah was having a late breakfast because she had arrived home exhausted, and alone with the syce, after one of the dinner parties. As she pushed the sliced mango around her plate, grateful that there was no animal emergency to have to deal with, she decided that the time had come to go and see Garth. The times they were alone together were further and fewer between. She simply must tell him that she really was finding that the parties were not enjoyable anymore if she had to go home alone.

She was absorbed in this thought when a toto came riding up the driveway. She stood up to see what he wanted, and he handed her a letter. She took it absentmindedly, giving him a sixpence for his trouble, expecting it would be another call for her to go to a sick animal. She gasped audibly as she read.

Dear Hannah,

I am back at last. Although I still have both my legs, it was a rough trip over. I am afraid that I am not feeling terribly well, yet, but I would love to see Sophie. Of course, I am looking forward to seeing you too, but perhaps the excitement would be a bit much for me just yet. If you would be so kind as to send Sophie over for a visit, or even to stay here, depending on how much you will miss her, I would be most grateful and I'm sure it would help to speed my recovery.

Yours as always,
Dan

"Dan's back. He hasn't heard. My letter was too late." She spoke out loud.

"Oh, well, if that's all it is," replied Mrs. Butler, who had come out to see who had arrived. "I thought it was something serious. You look like you've seen a ghost. Anyway, as I was saying last night about long engagements. . ."

Hannah wasn't listening. "I'll have to go and see him myself," she said.

"Yes, of course you will," Mrs. Butler responded. "You and Garth are the ones who have to set the date before anything else can really be done."

Hannah gave her mother a puzzled look and excused herself. She would go and see Dan right away. The less time she gave herself to think about it, the better. She sent a toto out to the stable with a message for the syce to saddle up Kindye at once.

The ride to Dan's was long and stressful. Hannah lived over and over again the moments after she heard of Sophie's death. She tried out different ways of telling Dan, sometimes confessing outright that it was all her fault, and other times making it sound as if it was only an unavoidable accident. By the time she came over the hill and saw the mission station in the valley below, nestled comfortably by a stream, surrounded by stately old thorn trees, she was in a state of utter turmoil. She reined Kindye in for a moment and tried to collect her thoughts. Why, oh why, hadn't she written sooner? None of this would be happening if she had. Just then a dog down at the station noticed the strange horse up on the hill and started barking. There was no turning back now. Hannah nudged Kindye and they headed downward.

She was surprised that Dan didn't come out to meet her. One of the schoolchildren came out instead and took Kindye. "Bwana's in the house," he explained, nodding toward the door of the little tin-roofed building off to the side of the large schoolhouse. Hannah took a deep breath to steady her nerves and went over to knock on the door. But the door was open.

"Hello," she called out hesitantly, peering into the gloom inside. There was a creaking noise, and as her eyes adjusted to the darkness, she saw a figure moving slowly towards her in a wheelchair.

"Hannah! What are you doing here? Did you bring Sophie with you?" The voice was thin and colorless and for a moment Hannah didn't recognize it as Dan's. She stood in the doorway, staring in horror.

"What happened? You never told me!" she blurted out.

"There was a war, Hannah. These things happen in a war, you know." Hannah was speechless. There was emotion to the voice now, but it was bitter and sarcastic. "I wanted you to send Sophie over, not to come yourself. Now, you see why."

There were a few moments of complete silence while Hannah tried to take in the sight before her. Dan's legs were thin and useless in the chair, but the most horrifying thing was the huge scar across his face. It sliced right from his chin, over the lips and up the right cheek to the temple, just missing the eye. "I'm so sorry, Dan," she managed to whisper.

Dan shrugged, "Don't be. I'll live."

"Sophie's dead," she blurted out quickly in case she gave in to the overwhelming urge she was feeling to turn and flee.

"What? Why didn't you tell me? When? How? What do you mean, dead?"

"I did tell you, Dan, but you must have left England before my letter arrived. I'm sorry, Dan, please forgive me. It was my fault. I accidentally let her follow me to Osbourne's and he thought she was a wild elephant and shot her. She was getting so big, you see. It was a terrible mistake. Please forgive me, Dan. I'm so sorry."

Dan's voice was cold and distant. "Come in here, Hannah,

and sit down. Explain what happened to me again; I don't quite understand."

Hannah came inside and repeated the whole story of Sophie's death. She sat at a small table opposite Dan, and he listened in total silence. The longer he was quiet, the more Hannah talked, desperate to get some kind of reaction from him, but he just stared at her while she babbled away. Finally, realizing how ridiculous she sounded repeating herself over and over again, she said, "That is the whole story, Dan. It was my fault. Please forgive me."

"There is just one thing I don't understand," replied Dan. "Why didn't you go and look for her if you knew she was missing?"

Hannah realized with a sinking feeling that she had been carefully avoiding mention of Garth, who was in fact the whole reason for her behavior on that day. She took a long, shuddering breath and plunged in.

"I was invited to a party at Garth Whitehead's house. His mother had just arrived from England, and he had invited me to meet her." Dan stared at her, as if there should be more to the story than that. "He asked me to marry him. We are engaged," she added lamely.

"Ah," replied Dan. "Well, thank you for coming. And congratulations on your engagement. I hope you'll be very happy. Good-bye." He turned his chair around and wheeled through a door on the far side of the room. Hannah stared after him for a moment. She could feel hot emotion rising up inside her, and she suddenly turned and rushed outside to find Kindye before she erupted into a rush of tears.

Hannah's ride back from the mission station was as unseeing as her ride out. At first she was blinded by the tears streaming down her face. The picture of Dan—broken, scarred, and ugly in the small, dark hut waiting for Sophie—

made her weep with sorrow. But the cold harshness of his voice had shocked her more, and then she wept for what the war had done to his mind and heart. Finally she remembered his abrupt dismissal of her and how he refused to answer her when she begged him for forgiveness, and she became angry. Furious even. He was a Christian, wasn't he? She wept tears of humiliation and frustration. What was the good of being a Christian if you treated people this way?

But as she got closer to home, she began to feel calmer. Her emotions were spent and she was drained. Her mind began to function again. She had heard reports of the terrible suffering the soldiers were experiencing in the war. How could she know what Dan had been put through over there in those trenches, watching his friends die and being in danger of dying every minute himself? And then to be wounded the way he was. How would he be able to carry on with his life's work and live in Africa when he couldn't even walk? And the scar across his face made him look hideous. Of course he wouldn't behave like the old Dan she used to know. How could he?

And then to find out so suddenly about Sophie. She remembered how devastated she had been when Sophie died, and she hadn't even been through a war. She couldn't expect Dan to take it well. She should have realized that. And to have to face her seeing him in the condition he was in would be humiliating for him. She should have understood that he didn't want to see her or he would have invited her over with Sophie. Any man would be embarrassed to be seen in such an incapacitated condition, especially a man who was used to being so independent.

Suddenly, she felt a twinge of guilt. It took her a couple of minutes to work out what was causing it. Dan was upset about her marrying Garth. She should have realized that he was beginning to have feelings for her by the way he wrote to her, but she was so preoccupied with Garth she didn't want to admit it to herself. Deep down she must have known; after all, that was why she didn't want to talk about why she had failed to look for Sophie when she knew she was missing. It was only when she told him about her engagement that he turned and left.

But as soon as Hannah had thought this through, she became angry. After all, she had a right to become engaged if she chose. She had never given Dan any kind of encouragement. They were just friends; she had never thought of him in any other way. He had no right to be upset about her engagement; in fact, he should be happy for her. Her anger acted on her like a bucket of cold water. All of a sudden she felt better. She was not the one at fault here. Dan was.

And what about his Christian duty to forgive her when she asked him to? What was the use of all this high-flown talk about forgiving one another if you only did it when you felt like it? She had apologized for what happened to Sophie, and after all, how was she to know that old Jack Osbourne would shoot her? It was, at least partly, just an accident, and Dan didn't have any right to treat her so contemptuously. So much for Christianity. Perhaps Rosie's magic charms worked better anyhow. After all, she was engaged now, even if it didn't bring her as much happiness as she thought it would.

By the time Hannah arrived back at the house, she was starving. It was well past lunchtime, so she would have to go around to the kitchen to see if there was anything in the pantry. Then she would head down to the clinic to see if anyone needed seeing to. Dan Williams was old news now. She was sorry for him, with all his injuries, but he was no longer any of her concern. And neither was that useless faith and prayer business that he used to be so proud of.

ten

Mrs. Butler met Hannah at the door in a state of high anxiety. "Good gracious, Hannah, where have you been? Don't you realize it is Garth's going-away party tonight? And look at the state you're in, filthy and tired and sunburnt! He will be gone for three months. The very least you could do is to look nice for him before he goes."

"Mother, there is plenty of time to get ready. And I really don't feel much like going anyway. There will be so many people there and I honestly don't feel like smiling and simpering all night." Hannah spoke without thinking.

"Hannah Butler! I really don't know what a man like Garth Whitehead sees in you, but since he sees something, you'd better at least try your best to fit in with his friends. They are the best of what little good society we have here and you simply must make an effort.

"And I think you and Garth should set a date for the wedding before he leaves. Lady Whitehead and I both need to know when to tell people to expect to come. I want you to mention it to him tonight. He won't be leaving for two more days, so you can make some sort of decision before then if you get him thinking seriously tonight. I want you to do that for me."

Hannah sighed and went through to the kitchen to ask that some hot water be prepared for her. This endless round of parties was turning out to be more work than running her veterinary practice. *But at least Garth will be gone in a couple of days and I'll have some peace,* she thought.

As she bathed and washed her hair for the evening, she found herself descending into a blacker and blacker mood. At first she decided that it was Dan's reaction to the news of Sophie that was upsetting her—that, and the fact that Garth was going to be gone for three months. But the more she thought about her life these days, the more she realized it was more than that. She was feeling frustrated that she was being pressured by her mother into setting a date for the wedding. Surely it wasn't supposed to be this way. The prospective groom shouldn't be avoiding the wedding, should he?

Her hair was still wet and she was still in her housecoat, but she was feeling so low at the thought of Garth avoiding the wedding that she sank down onto her bed and lay without moving. As she thought about it, she realized Garth wasn't just advoiding the wedding he was advoiding her, too. She could hardly remember the last time they had had any time alone together. The only time she saw him these days was at parties, endless parties. And she usually went home with her mother. What had she gotten herself involved in? Her wildest dreams had become reality and they were turning out to be nightmares.

There was a rap on the door. "Hannah? Are you nearly ready?" Mrs. Butler's voice jarred her peace.

"Yes, give me a few more minutes, Mother. It won't matter if we are late."

Hannah sighed and dutifully swung her feet to the floor and began to brush out her hair. Her mother was right. She wasn't as pretty or bubbly as all the other girls Garth knew. What did he see in her? At first she thought it was because they both loved horses, but they hardly spent any time with his horses anymore. Garth seemed to have lost interest in racing. All he thought about now was safaris and making money. Maybe he had lost interest in her too. The thought sent a chill through her heart. Being engaged to Garth wasn't turning out to be the joy she had thought it would be, but perhaps it was her fault. Perhaps if she could just try a little harder to be like the other girls, then Garth would remember how he had loved her and things would go back to the way they were at the beginning. Yes, she decided, setting her face like flint, she would try harder. She wished she hadn't thrown away the cowrie shell Rosie had given her.

Later that evening when Hannah and Mrs. Butler arrived at the Whiteheads', the twinkling lights and the music and all the horses and surreys lined up outside the stately old place sent a shaft of fear into Hannah's heart. Surely, this was not where she belonged. She was much more at home in the stables, with the animals. She wanted to turn and run, but it was far too late for that now. She had to face what she had gotten herself into.

As she ascended the steps up to the veranda with her mother on her arm, she caught a glimpse of Garth chatting with some ladies in front of the window. They were all laughing and giggling. Hannah could tell that Garth was teasing the prettiest one about something by the way she blushed and nodded her head so that the ringlets that framed her pink cheeks bobbed up and down. Garth smiled indulgently down at her and Hannah wondered if he had ever looked at her that way. She doubted it.

As they entered the room, Lady Whitehead spotted them and came over to greet them. "Hannah, my dear, and Florence. How lovely to see you. May I take your shawls? Juma, please fetch the ladies a glass of wine." She linked her arms through both of theirs and drew them into the party. Hannah glanced over her shoulder. Garth was still talking to the group of ladies. He hadn't noticed that she had arrived. This was so very unlike the first party he had invited her to, where he had proposed. What had she done to let things go so far wrong?

"Hannah! How are you?" Hannah turned and saw Fiona Brown smiling beside her.

"Oh, hello, Fiona. It's nice to see you. You are looking very well."

"Thank you, Hannah." She smiled warmly and Hannah was grateful that Fiona was her friend.

Mrs. Butler had moved on to another group of guests once Fiona had begun to converse with Hannah. But in the moment of silence that followed, a familiar voice cut through the rest of the party buzz. Hannah looked up to find that Leticia was standing a few feet away with her back to them, regaling a group of her friends with something she felt strongly about.

"Yes, it simply wouldn't do to have your fiancée working out in the stables amongst all the animals and the dirt and what have you. I can't imagine what Garth thought he was doing! Well, I hope they will be very happy." She glanced significantly over at Garth, who was animatedly chatting with another group of ladies.

Hannah wished she could crawl under a couch and hide. She was never very good at playing the games that other women played with each other. She suddenly felt overwhelmed with longing for Sophie, and tears came to her eyes. Luckily, Leticia was sweeping off in the direction of Garth and his group of ladies. Hannah took two or three steps backwards as if she had been hit and fortunately bumped into a settee, where she sank down gratefully. Fiona, looking concerned, quickly sat down beside her. Hannah wished she would go away so she could be alone for a moment, but Fiona's voice was sympathetic when she spoke.

"Never mind Leticia, Hannah. She is only jealous. After

all, Garth is quite a catch, or so people think."

Hannah was grateful for the kind tone of Fiona's voice, but she was too overcome to say anything. She sat quietly for a moment, then looked up and saw Garth, who finally looked her way. He excused himself and came over to greet her.

"Hannah, my dear. You slipped in without my noticing." He bent over and kissed her on the cheek. "Hello, Fiona! How are you?" Fiona merely nodded in response, but Garth didn't seem to be offended.

"What's the matter, Hannah? Your eyes are rather blood-shot and your face is all red. Did you drive too fast and catch a bit too much wind? Perhaps you'd better retire to the powder room for a few minutes and fix up your face. You wouldn't want people to see you looking so disheveled.

"Leticia, how are you?" Garth suddenly caught sight of Leticia as she sidled back over to Hannah's side. "I haven't seen you for ages. My, my you're looking even lovelier than I remember!" He bent over and whispered into Hannah's ear. "Just pop over to the bedroom for a few minutes and powder your nose." Without missing a beat, he straightened up and took Leticia's arm. "Let me fetch you a glass of wine."

Hannah looked after him in horror.

"Come with me, Hannah." It was Fiona. She took Hannah's elbow and steered her out of the room and into the garden. "Let's walk out here for a few minutes until you feel better," she said as they stepped onto the soft dewy grass of the front lawn. Although the sounds of the party bubbled away behind them, Hannah was immensely grateful for the quietness of the garden.

"Thank you, Fiona," she whispered. They walked along the edge of the lawn in silence. A few tree frogs croaked in the night air and cicadas buzzed lazily around them. There was the odd bird that dared compete with the noise of the party, and a guest's horse whinnied impatiently now and then, but to Hannah it was blessed silence.

After they had made a complete circuit of the lawn and were about to start another one, Hannah's emotions became too powerful to contain any longer. She felt she must tell someone what she had been thinking. There was no one else but Fiona. It was a humiliating admission, but she simply felt she must tell someone, and Fiona understood trouble.

"Fiona, I must tell you something," Hannah blurted out suddenly. Fiona looked at her and Hannah was grateful to see that she didn't look shocked, only sympathetic. "Fiona, I think I have made a terrible mistake by becoming engaged to Garth." She sighed audibly. Just saying the thought aloud lifted a huge burden from her shoulders. She waited for Fiona's reply, but there was only silence as the two of them followed their first set of footprints around the wet lawn. The silence stretched out for a long time, and Hannah thought she had made another mistake in speaking aloud when finally Fiona responded.

"Hannah, I have been praying for you." This was not the response Hannah was waiting for. The picture of Dan rolling angrily out the door in his wheelchair that morning flashed into Hannah's mind at the mention of prayer. Hannah groaned aloud.

"I'm sorry, Hannah, I didn't mean to offend you," Fiona said. "Only there is something I learned about only last week and I feel very uncertain about whether or not I should mention it to you. And I prayed for some guidance." She paused. Hannah didn't have anything to say. She didn't feel she could handle any more emotionally wrenching news today, but she had a sinking feeling that it would be better to find out and get it over with.

Fiona continued, "Anyway, after seeing how things are for you tonight, I feel that perhaps the Lord is leading me to say something, if you don't mind." She waited for Hannah to reply.

"Go on," Hannah said reluctantly and steeled herself to listen.

"Jim and Garth were talking about the safari business that they are starting up. I was writing letters in the bedroom and the house was very quiet, so I overheard their conversation. It seems that Lady Whitehead had told Garth that she wouldn't support his gambling any longer and that he had to settle down and get married or she would withhold his allowance."

Hannah blushed with shame. Even though she hadn't admitted it even to herself, she hadn't really forgotten the letter from his mother she had seen on Garth's table that day long ago. So, Garth did have an ulterior motive in marrying her. How could she have been so unbelievably stupid and naïve?

"Anyway, Hannah," Fiona went on, "I feel just awful telling you this. I know it is none of my business, but I hate to see you hurt and humiliated in front of people like Leticia, so I just want you to know that Garth told Jim that he was only going to stay engaged to you for as long as his mother was visiting and once she was gone he would break it off with you. By then he and Jim thought they would be making enough with their safari business, so if Lady Whitehead cut Garth off it wouldn't matter."

Fiona was speaking quickly now, rushing to get everything out in the open before Hannah could react. "I'm so sorry, Hannah, but I know how difficult it is to be married to a non-Christian man, and so I just wanted to save you some awful heartache. I hope you won't hold this against me."

Hannah was still thinking about the letter. They came to a bench in a dark corner of the garden, and Hannah sat heavily down. She was having so much trouble even finding the energy to stand up this evening. "I know, Fiona," she said, putting her head into her hands. "I've known all along, but I was just too stupid and vain to admit it."

Fiona put her arm around Hannah's shoulders. "I'm so sorry, Hannah," she said softly. As they sat there in the evening quietness and coolness, Hannah knew what she must do. She was grateful to have Fiona there because she wouldn't be able to back out of her plan once she had told someone.

"I read a letter that Garth had left out from his mother," she began. Fiona listened quietly. "It was ages ago, before Garth asked me to marry him, but I chose not to think about it. It was very stupid of me, but you know how Garth is. He can make you feel like you are the only person who exists for him, and I got caught in his spell. Actually, I chose to think that he was caught in mine." Hannah laughed bitterly at the thought of how she had tried to capture Garth with the magic shell. She had been caught in her own web.

"Thank you, Fiona. You are a real friend to me, and now I know what I must do." Hannah stood up. The heaviness that had weighed her down like a stone all night was slowly lifting and a sense of resolve energized her mind. Fiona stood up too. Together they walked towards the party, making a new path of wet footprints right across the middle of the lawn and up the steps of the veranda.

Hannah spotted Garth regaling a group of friends with stories of adventure and fortune to be had in the world of big-game hunting. Mrs. Butler caught sight of Hannah as she strode towards the center of the room.

"Hannah, there you are. Where have you been? I've been looking everywhere for you. Lady Whitehead wants to ask you about—"

"Not now, Mother! I have to speak to Garth."

Mrs. Butler dropped away from her daughter's side, but

she looked after her nervously.

"Garth, I need to speak to you. Now." Hannah announced as she approached the group. He turned and looked at her, irritated with the intrusion.

"Hannah, I'm in the middle of a story, if you don't mind. And look at your shoes. What are you doing trekking all that wet grass in here?"

Hannah noticed Leticia, who was standing next to Garth, smirking with amusement at the scene she was creating. Steel entered her mind.

"Garth, I need to speak to you now," she repeated.

Garth turned and faced her again, but this time he was angry. Mrs. Butler rushed up and tugged on Hannah's elbow. "Hannah, what do you think you are doing? Come away. Behave yourself."

Hannah shook her mother off. "Fine, Garth, if you won't talk to me alone, we'll talk here. I am breaking off our engagement. I know you have never intended to marry me. You don't even have time to speak to me in private anymore."

There was a collective gasp and Mrs. Butler shrieked. Garth stepped forward and put his hands on Hannah's shoulders. "Come now, Han, old chap, you're just overwrought. I'm sorry; I have been awfully preoccupied these days, and I admit I have shamefully neglected you. But there is no need to be so upset. Come with me; we'll just go to my study and sort it all out." He slipped one arm around Hannah's shoulder and tried to lead her towards the door, but she planted her feet like a balky colt.

"No, Garth, there is nothing to sort out. I know you are only engaged to me because of your mother. I know what you are up to. Now let go of me. I'm going home."

Garth stepped back, his face darkening with fury. "How dare you stand here in my home and accuse me like this in front of my guests." His voice cut like glass and his lips were pulled tightly back against his teeth. Hannah suddenly felt afraid, but she turned away to leave.

She had taken only one step when her shoulder was wrenched backwards and she was spun around to face Garth's raging anger.

"You little strumpet! You are the one that used me. You followed me around like a little puppy, begging me to pay attention to you, begging me to kiss you, and practically throwing yourself at me. I didn't notice you showing any reluctance to marry me, and now you have the audacity to use me like this in front of my mother and my guests. You are the one who has treated me shamefully." He suddenly turned to face the horrified guests. "She has used me, I tell you!"

Lady Whitehead was galvanized into action. "Garth, be quiet this instant!" Her voice wasn't loud, but the conviction with which she spoke silenced her son. He looked at her for a moment, stunned, and then turned tail and fled out of the front door.

This was the cue for Mrs. Butler to let out another shriek and faint dramatically into the surprised arms of a young man standing behind her. Hannah glanced at her mother, then back into the still-smirking face of Leticia. That was the last straw. She followed Garth to the door, where he had brushed rudely past Fiona.

"Fiona, would you be so kind as to give me a lift home?" Hannah was surprised at the strength and confidence of her own voice.

"By all means," Fiona answered, and the two of them walked arm in arm down the steps of the veranda, out into the warm welcome of the frogs and insects and away from the shock and disdain behind them.

eleven

"How could you embarrass me like that, in front of Lady Whitehead, in front of all my friends, everybody who is anybody in this town!" Mrs. Butler shrieked as she burst into Hannah's room, catching her daughter as she slipped into bed. Her face was red with rage. Hannah faced her with a cold calmness.

"Mother, he was using me. Using me for money. Doesn't that make you angry?" Hannah suddenly saw her mother as a self-centered, fearful, lonely woman, not the raging, awe-inspiring, powerful woman she had feared for so long. She was amazed at herself for being so blind for all these years.

"I don't care!" spluttered Mrs. Butler, still livid. "I don't care what he was doing. You had no right to wash your dirty laundry in front of everyone in town. There are other ways to deal with men like that, and if you weren't so incorrigible, you would have seen that you could have used him in return. What did you think? He was put on Earth to cater to your whims?"

Her newfound ability to see through her mother gave Hannah an advantage. "Mother," she said firmly, "I will not be used like that. I doubt there was anyone else in that room who was surprised at what I said except you and me. And I don't need anything Garth Whitehead has. I am perfectly capable of supporting us both with my work."

"You are the most selfish child in the world! What do you think it is like for me to have to live with a spinster daughter and no grandchildren and, worst of all, absolutely no social standing whatsoever? What do you think it is like for me?

Have you ever given a thought to the feelings of your poor mother? Or do you only think of yourself? What did I ever do wrong when I raised you? I should have stood up to your father. He spoiled you. Spoiled you completely, and now I have to suffer the consequences!" She turned and stormed out, slamming Hannah's door so hard the mirror on the back of it came crashing down.

Hannah went over to pick up the mirror. There was a large crack down the length of it, but it hadn't shattered. Automatically, her mother's voice came to mind, "It's bad luck to break a mirror."

"Luck. Magic." Hannah spoke the words aloud. It seemed that all her life she had been surrounded by superstition. It was bad luck to have been used so badly by Garth, but she had tried to lure him to her with magic. Everything was an illusion with one of them trying to control the other without the other one knowing. What a dishonest, unfair way to treat each other. How could she have mistaken it for love?

Dan's face slipped uninvited into her mind, as it did so often. Dan was the one who spoke of love. He seemed to think he knew what love was about. It was about God and prayer. But God didn't answer her prayers, so how could He love her?

Hannah crawled into bed again. She went on puzzling it out in her mind as she lay there in the darkness. If God had answered her prayer, she wouldn't have had to go to Rosie. She wouldn't have become engaged to Garth and she wouldn't have been used so shamefully by him.

And what about Sophie? If she hadn't just prayed for her, then gone rushing off to Garth's, Sophie might still be alive. Could she really expect God to answer her prayers when her own actions didn't correspond to what she was praying for? Perhaps she had been mistaken about God. Perhaps she should have been paying more attention to what she thought were unanswered prayers instead of being so intent on getting her own way by whatever means she could come up with. Perhaps it was time to change the way she thought about things. And with that in mind, Hannah fell into a deep and exhausted sleep.

She was awakened abruptly in the morning by a loud knock at her door. Without waiting for a reply, her mother strode in. She was still in her dressing gown and carried an envelope in her hand.

"This just arrived from Lady Whitehead for you. Open it." Mrs. Butler's voice was cold and angry this morning, but she was obviously overcome with curiosity.

Hannah struggled to sit up and wake up, trying to remember everything that had happened the night before. She took the letter from her mother's hand and tore it open.

My dear Hannah,

I am writing to tell you how sorry I am to be losing you as a future daughter-in-law. I am deeply sorry for the way my son has treated you. I was rather afraid that that may be the case, which is why I encouraged you to take your time with the engagement. However, I confess I didn't want to admit to myself that he would do such a thing and I hoped that you and he were in love. You would have made a wonderful wife for him if he had treated you well, and I am sorry to lose you.

I will be returning home to England as soon as I can secure a passage on a ship. I wish you all the best of luck in your future.

Yours sincerely,
Lady Whitehead

Hannah silently handed the letter to her mother, who had been waiting impatiently for her to read it. Mrs. Butler took it, read it, and threw it down on Hannah's bed. Snorting angrily, she stalked out of the room. Hannah lay back down with a sigh.

Later, after breakfasting in silence with her mother, Hannah walked to the clinic feeling lighter and more content than she had for a long time. She would throw herself into her work, she decided. That had been the way she had dealt with the difficulties in her life up until now, and it had worked fairly well. There would be only one thing different and that would be that she would stay away from superstition. That was what had gotten her into trouble, and she would keep away from it.

The morning light slanted through the trees onto the damp, dewy road. Everything felt fresh and new, like the dawning of a new world. Birds were singing loudly, and Hannah felt it had been ages since she had heard them. Her mind had been so filled with Garth—first the all-consuming daydreams, then counting the hours when she would see him, wondering what he was thinking, analyzing how he had treated her the night before, and wondering how he would treat her that night. It was such a relief to be a part of the real world again—to feel the morning sun, listen to the birds, and look forward to a day of doing something worthwhile.

But as she drew closer to the clinic, she felt a certain emptiness. She still missed Sophie. She felt badly that Dan was so angry with her. If only she could go back to the way things were before she had become involved with Garth. She had spoiled so much. Or rather, she had let him spoil things for her.

She hadn't been long at the clinic before a note arrived for her. It was from Fiona, asking her to meet her for lunch in town, and at noon Hannah duly set out for the Kikuru tea-house where Fiona suggested they meet. Fiona was there, waiting at a table, when Hannah arrived. She rose excitedly when she saw her.

"Hannah, how are you today? I'm so glad you could come!"

Hannah pulled off her hat as she went over to Fiona's table, and wished she had gone home first and dressed up a little more. Fiona had on a light blue cotton dress and a small straw hat with a blue ribbon around it, and she looked so young and fresh. But it was too late to change now. *Besides,* she reminded herself, *I no longer need to impress anyone.* Nevertheless, she could feel a hostile glare boring into her from behind. Glancing up, she caught the image of Leticia in a mirror behind Fiona. She hadn't noticed her when she came in, sitting by the window staring at her with a look of amused contempt. Hannah focused her eyes on Fiona's welcoming face.

"Hello, Fiona. Thank you for inviting me. I'm afraid I didn't have time to go home to change into something nicer."

"Good heavens, this isn't Nairobi. Sit down and relax!"

Hannah sat down gratefully, and they ordered some sandwiches for lunch.

"I'm so glad you could come to lunch with me," began Fiona, leaning forward to speak to Hannah quietly. "I was worried about you after last night, and I just wanted to be sure you are alright."

"Yes, I'm just fine, thanks," Hannah replied. "I feel better than I have in weeks. I am very grateful to you for telling me what you knew about Garth. I only feel embarrassed to have been so gullible. I really made an awful fool of myself in front of all of Kikuru."

"I'm sorry it happened like that, Hannah. But you know, I

admire you for facing up to it the way you did. And Garth deserved to be shown up like that in front of all his friends for what he did to you. He should be ashamed of himself."

The waiter brought cucumber sandwiches and set them in front of Hannah and Fiona. Hannah looked down at the little crustless triangles, nestled between a sprig of parsley and a couple of slices of tomato. She was starving and these lady-like little morsels would hardly keep her going for an hour. She wished she had ordered the plate of roast beef, but it had seemed so unladylike at the time. Still, she would have to get over trying to be ladylike at meals while working at a man's job all day. She sighed and started slowly, trying to make the sandwiches last.

"I do love to come here for lunch," Fiona was saying. "They make the most delicious sandwiches. The bread is so light and fresh and their pastries are just delicious, don't you think?"

Hannah was caught with her mouth full, but she nodded and finally managed to say, "I don't really know. It has been such a long time since I have taken lunch in town."

"Oh, dear, we'll have to do this more often then," Fiona responded, but Hannah could tell that her eyes were following someone else behind her. She winced, guessing who it may be.

"Hannah Butler!" came Leticia's shrill voice, and Hannah knew she had been right. "Well, I see you are out on the town already. Your broken heart heals very quickly, doesn't it?" Leticia's smile was brittle and icy.

"Leticia, I don't think you have any right to judge Hannah's actions," Fiona spoke up angrily. Leticia glared at her.

"Fiona Brown! Why, I didn't notice you. Is Hannah unable to speak for herself, poor thing?"

Sarcasm dripped off Leticia's words like icicles, and Hannah turned crimson with rage. She stood up, knocking her chair down and drawing the attention of everyone in the cafe.

"Why don't you marry him, Leticia? You would be just what he deserves." Hannah surprised herself with the vehemence of her voice, and obviously she must have surprised Leticia too. There was a pin-dropping silence while everyone waited for Leticia to reply. Leticia's face turned pink and then white.

"You are obviously upset because he was losing interest in you. I can assure you, if I had wanted to marry him, he wouldn't have lost interest in me." She spun around and swept out the door. The waiter scurried around the tables and set Hannah's chair up again. Hannah sat down, feeling the eyes of everyone in the room on her back, but in a minute the buzz of voices resumed like ripples of water in a pool covering the spot where a stone had just landed. Fiona reached out and took Hannah's hand.

"Well done, Hannah. You put her in her place. I didn't know you were so good at that sort of thing!" Hannah was surprised to hear a note of admiration in Fiona's voice.

"Neither did I," she replied, "but she had the last word."

"Never mind. She is not the kind of person you would choose for a friend, so I wouldn't worry about her opinion." Fiona paused, and Hannah could tell she wanted to say something else. "I was wondering, Hannah, if you would be interested in joining some of us at the church. We meet once a week to pray for our soldiers in Europe, and we also put together boxes of food and clothes to send to the soldiers in the trenches."

Fiona rushed on, speaking quickly to get all her thoughts out before Hannah could say no. "I notice that you and your mother come to church quite often these days, and I also hear that you and Dan Williams at the mission station are friends, so I thought maybe you would like to join us in doing church work. I thought it would be a good way for us to become better friends; that is, if you would like to become better friends with me." She stopped speaking suddenly and looked anxiously at Hannah.

Hannah was silent. There was something she wasn't quite sure about, and she wanted to ask Fiona. But it was an awkward question.

"Well, that sounds like a good cause," Hannah said haltingly, "only—well, I don't know if I would fit in properly. You say you pray for the men every week. I'm not sure about praying, you see. I haven't done that sort of thing before very much and I don't know if I. . .well, I'm just not sure. . ."

"Oh, Hannah, I don't mean to offend you," Fiona jumped in quickly. "I know we don't know each other very well. Perhaps I should tell you a little about myself first.

"When I came to live in Kikuru three years ago after Jim and I were married, I began to attend the church here. I never really gave much thought to my faith before, but I didn't know anyone here and the people I met at church were very welcoming and friendly. I joined the ladies' prayer group and I learned that Jesus had died for my sins. I could pray to Him and He would hear my prayers.

"At first I didn't know how important that was that I could pray, but as you know, my marriage to Jim has had its difficulties with him spending all his money on horses and racing. I turned to Jesus and asked Him to help me. And He did. I could feel His presence with us when we had no money. Always something would turn up to prevent us from starving. Even though we had to sell our farm to pay Jim's debts, Jim got work as a farm manager out on the Suffolk Estate. That was a real answer to prayer, and we will be able to start afresh. I think Jim was really shaken to his foundations when he lost the farm. I know I was. It has made him pay attention to God." Fiona paused and looked down at her plate, and when she looked up again, Hannah could see that her face was flushed with pleasure.

"I learned last week that we are expecting a baby. We had been hoping for news like this ever since we were married and we were beginning to worry that we would never be able to have a family. Jim was so happy. I don't think I had ever seen him so happy since we got married. I really think God is answering my prayers for Jim and he will become a Christian through all this.

"Then yesterday when he learned Garth's reasons for becoming engaged to you, I think his friendship with Garth was quite shaken. Last night after we drove you home, he was very concerned for you and actually, it was he who suggested I ask you to join our ladies' prayer group.

"Anyway, Hannah, please excuse me for telling you all these personal things, but I thought we might become friends and you may be interested in Christian things."

Hannah was thinking hard. Everything was happening so quickly. Everywhere she turned, she was being met by Christians who wanted her to pray and trust in Jesus. She was beginning to feel that she should trust, but there were still some things she didn't really understand. She didn't know if she really was able to tell anyone about them. It was still too new to put into her own words yet.

"I am so happy to hear you are expecting a baby," she said at last, buying herself a few more moments.

"Thank you. I am grateful to God for giving me such news at such a time."

"Fiona, it is so strange that you are asking me to join the prayer group. It seems to me that everywhere I turn these days, I am meeting up with God, or at least someone who wants to tell me about Him."

Fiona smiled broadly. "He is trying to reach you, and is already working in your life, Hannah."

"Well, I'm not terribly certain that is true, Fiona. There are some things that I have done and I don't think He is very pleased with me." As she spoke to Fiona, Hannah began to feel the need to tell her about Sophie. There was no one who knew but Dan, and he was so angry. It would be such a relief to tell someone who understood what had happened to Sophie. She blurted out the whole story while Fiona sat quietly and listened. Then she came to the part where she had tried to ask Dan to forgive her.

"He just turned and wheeled his chair out of the room," she explained, and suddenly Hannah felt her eyes filling with tears. It was not the part about Sophie that was making her cry anymore, but suddenly she realized what Dan meant to her. "He won't forgive me, Fiona, and how can I know that God will forgive me if he won't? I know I was wrong and I did pray for forgiveness, but I don't feel that anyone has forgiven me. And I haven't forgiven myself either, especially when I learned that Garth was just using me, and Sophie died for nothing!" Hannah's voice choked and she took her napkin and wiped her eyes.

Fiona reached over the table to take her hand again. "Hannah, I'm so sorry. I'm so sorry about Sophie and about Dan too. But Dan is only a man. He is not God; remember that. Even if Dan hasn't forgiven you, remember that God does forgive you." She reached into her bag and brought out a tiny Bible, worn and frayed around the edges. Hannah wondered how she could possibly read such tiny print, but Fiona flipped the little book open to a page and began to read. "If we confess our sins, he is faithful and just to forgive us our sins." She paused and looked at Hannah. "You confessed to God what happened to Sophie, Hannah, so you can be certain God has forgiven you. The only unforgiven sins are unconfessed ones."

"But Dan is a Christian. Aren't Christians supposed to forgive?" Hannah asked.

"Yes, they are, but Christians aren't always perfect. I am surprised that Dan treated you that way, Hannah. I have always heard the most wonderful things about him and the work he is doing. All I can think of is that the war was very hard on him, and he isn't quite himself yet. You know there is terrible suffering over there in the trenches. Men come back broken in body and in spirit. Perhaps something very bad happened to Dan and he is having trouble coping with it. That is why I believe it is so important that we pray for the poor men who are over in Europe fighting to end war forever."

"Yes, perhaps you are right," Hannah replied slowly, "but if God has forgiven me, then why don't I feel as though He has? I don't feel that He has even heard me."

"Hannah, it is not the way you feel that is important. It is what God says that is important. God cares about how you feel, but you can't go around making decisions based on feelings. You make decisions based on God's Word and then God takes care of your feelings. Think about what happened with Garth. Garth used your feelings to trap you. You must use a more reliable guide than your feelings to live your life. And you are forgiven by God; your feelings will come around later.

"Perhaps it would be helpful to you for us to meet together now and then to study the Bible so you understand what God is saying to you."

Hannah nodded. Their sandwiches were finished and the waiter had taken away their plates. Fiona paid the bill. "My treat," she explained. "Jim is not gambling anymore, so I can afford a few little things now." She smiled and took Hannah by the elbow as they left the cafe. It was almost empty now, Hannah noticed gratefully, thinking of her meeting with Leticia.

The two women parted on the street after making arrangements for Hannah to come to Fiona and Jim's new home in town the following evening.

As Hannah rode slowly back to the clinic, she thought over what Fiona had said. Perhaps she was right about Dan. After all, he had suffered and he had seen others die horribly in the trenches. Her heart went out to him. She wished she had been a little kinder and more patient with him when she had told him about Sophie. She remembered his smiling blue eyes looking down at her before he had gone off to war and tears came to her eyes again. She let them flow down her cheeks, making dirty wet tracks in her skin as they mingled with the dust from the road.

"Oh Lord, if You have really forgiven me for letting Sophie die, please let Dan forgive me too. I love him, Lord." She caught her breath at the words she had prayed. She had told God about what she felt for Dan before she had even admitted it to herself. But it was too late for Dan now. Even if he managed to forgive her, how could he ever come to like or respect her again after what she had done? Not only had she neglected Sophie, but she had chased after Garth so shamelessly. Kindye turned the corner and the clinic came into view. Hannah pulled a dirty handkerchief out of her pocket and wiped her face. It was time to face the rest of her life.

twelve

The days followed each other more quickly than Hannah dared to hope. She had plunged herself into her work, visiting sick animals on farms and seeing others in her clinic from morning to night. She spent a lot of time at Fiona and Jim's as well. Jim had joined her and Fiona in the little Bible studies that Fiona was doing for her to help her learn the basic truths of her new faith. She could see the happiness radiating around the couple as they bent over the table reading and talking with her, and her heart felt full with both joy for them and sorrow that she wouldn't see Dan again, that he hadn't forgiven her, that she hadn't treated him kindly when she had had the chance. But she tried hard not to think about him.

She tried to avoid her mother as much as she could. Mrs. Butler hadn't forgiven her either, but that was only to be expected. Surprisingly, Lady Whitehead had been very understanding. She had called in for tea a few days after the fateful party, just the day before she left on her way back to England. Mrs. Butler had apologized so profusely for her daughter's behavior that Lady Whitehead had hardly been able to get a word in edgewise as they sat drinking tea on the veranda. Hannah had wanted to jump up and shout at her mother to be quiet, but Lady Whitehead had looked over and given her a kindly but knowing look.

When at last Mrs. Butler paused for breath, Lady Whitehead addressed Hannah, "My dear Hannah, I have enjoyed getting to know you these last few months and I am terribly sorry about how abominably Garth has treated you." Mrs. Butler gasped in horror, but Lady Whitehead quickly continued.

"I'm afraid it was partly my fault, and I just want to apologize to you personally. As you know, Garth and I have had our differences, but I was hoping he would settle down. However, it was wrong of me to try to bribe him into doing so. My only regret is that he isn't good enough to fall in love with a sensible young woman like yourself. I know you would have made him a wonderful wife, and my wish is that one day you will make some other lucky young man very happy." She put her teacup down on the table in front of her.

"Oh, dear Lady Whitehead! How could you say such a thing! Garth is a wonderful young man. A little bit wild, but he will settle down soon." Mrs. Butler was bubbling over herself trying to mend unbroken fences between Hannah and Lady Whitehead, but Lady Whitehead simply smiled warmly at Hannah and picked up her sunshade.

"I must go, Mrs. Butler," she interrupted. "I have so much packing to see to before my train leaves tomorrow. Thank you so much for tea." She turned to Hannah and bent forward to kiss her cheek. "Good-bye, my dear; all the best to you in your future." And she slipped away down the steps and into her waiting surrey before Mrs. Butler could catch her breath. By the time she turned to face her daughter, Hannah had slipped inside and gone to her own bedroom to get ready to go back to work.

Two Sunday afternoons later Hannah was just finishing her lunch with her mother after they had come back from church. Hannah was debating her afternoon's activities in her mind. She wished God hadn't decreed that people should rest on the Sabbath. That meant a whole afternoon of her mother's company. She wanted to go to the clinic and work. Perhaps a farmer would have an emergency and she would have to attend to it, but that wasn't likely. She was just deciding that she would go out to the stables and saddle Kindye up for a ride when she caught sight of a figure riding up the driveway. *Oh, thank goodness,* she thought. *Someone needs a vet.* But she didn't recognize the figure. She waited until he came fully into view from out of the trees, and when she saw Dan Williams riding slowly up to the veranda she blinked with surprise. Her heart stopped beating for an instant, and she thought she must be imagining the sight. But Mrs. Butler wasn't.

"Good heavens, it's that missionary man again! I thought he had gone off to fight in the war. What is he doing here? I hope he doesn't have another elephant to foist upon you."

Hannah ran out to meet him, but then stopped short a few yards away, remembering how it had been the last time she saw him.

"Hannah!" he said, and she smiled with relief. Then she noticed the crutches strapped across his back like a gun. Awkwardly, he climbed down from his horse and transferred himself to the crutches. Hannah wanted desperately to help him, but she was still afraid he would be angry with her.

"Hannah, I'm so glad you are here. Would you mind walking with me for a few minutes? I need to speak to you alone, if you don't mind." Hannah was taken aback. His voice was not the way she remembered, stuttering and shy. He spoke with a calm determination. She walked over to his side, and they started slowly across the lawn. Mrs. Butler was calling out from the veranda.

"Hannah, where are you going? Hannah!" But to Hannah, she might have been a million miles away; she only heard Dan.

"Hannah," he was saying. He was trying to look into her

face, but it was her turn to be shy, and she kept her eyes on the lawn at their feet. "Hannah, I behaved very, very badly when you came to see me a few weeks ago. I would like to apologize to you. It was shameful of me to treat you that way. Please accept my deepest apology. I am sorry, Hannah."

They reached a path that wound through the trees at the bottom of the garden. It was too narrow for them to walk side by side with Dan on his crutches, so Hannah paused. Dan glanced quickly back at the house, where Mrs. Butler was standing on the veranda, her hands on her hips, watching them angrily. He nodded to the path, indicating that Hannah go first. Tentatively, Hannah began walking into the cool, soft shade of the huge trees. The cool air soothed her hot, red face, and she was relieved that Dan could no longer try to catch her eye. But the silence between them was heavy, and it was Dan who broke it again.

"Hannah," the authority in his voice stopped her in her tracks, and she turned to look at him. "Hannah, I don't deserve it after the way I treated you, but I feel so ashamed of losing your friendship that way after all you did for me while I was gone. Your letters meant so much to me and I don't deserve your forgiveness, but I need to know if you will accept my sincere apology for the way I behaved."

"Oh, Dan, of course I accept your apology! It is I who needs to apologize to you for letting Sophie get away. It is I who needs to be forgiven by you!" The smile that Hannah saw forming in Dan's eyes drew her forward. She reached out to touch his arm, but instantly his eyes became as hard as glass, and Hannah pulled away as if she had touched a live coal. She turned away and walked quickly down the path, glad it was so narrow. She could hear Dan hurrying along behind her on his crutches.

"Hannah! Wait!" She stopped, but she didn't turn around.

"Hannah, I must go now." His voice was still as hard as that last look in his eyes, and Hannah cringed as he spoke. "I am grateful to you for looking after Sophie and I have only thanks and gratitude to you for all you did so graciously. Thank you for accepting my apology, Hannah. Now before I go, I just want to offer you and your fiancé my best wishes, and may God bless you richly in your marriage. Good-bye, Hannah." How could he not know that she was no longer engaged! She turned to face him, but he was already heading away from her.

"Dan!" He kept going, and she realized her voice had only been a whisper. She ran after him and caught his arm. "Dan, I broke off the engagement weeks ago, after I saw you." He turned and looked at her. She couldn't read the new look in his eyes. She had never seen anyone look that way at her before, but it had a powerful effect on her. She wanted to laugh and cry at the same time.

"Hannah," his voice was shy and hesitant again, the way she remembered from before he went to war.

"Yes, Dan," she was still whispering.

"If I put my crutches down, will you take my arm and help me to walk without them?"

"Yes, Dan." And she took his arm and felt his weight bear down on her, but she stood firm and they took a step down the path.

"Hannah, I'm going to learn to walk again." He spoke slowly, his concentration on taking one step and then another. Hannah could feel his breath in her hair and she moved closer to support him more. She couldn't speak; the feel of his presence so close to her overwhelmed her. It was a far deeper and more intimate sensation than she ever remembered when she was near Garth. She suddenly realized Dan wasn't so much concentrating on walking; he was concentrating on her. She caught her breath, and she knew Dan had noticed. He stopped and turned, putting his hands on her shoulders.

"Hannah, I have another confession." He looked deeply into her eyes, but this time she couldn't turn away and hide; she was transfixed. "Hannah, I have fallen in love with you. You needn't answer me yet, but I need to know if I could ever hope that one day you might love me too. I have prayed and prayed that the Lord would help me to look upon you as just a dear friend, and I thought your engagement was my answer from Him. But now you are free and I cannot help myself from asking if there would ever be any hope for me. Of course, Hannah, you understand that if you take me into your life, you also take Jesus into your life too. If you can't have us both, then there is no hope for me." After such a long speech he stopped suddenly, hope and fear mingled together in his face.

Hannah could hardly take it in. After all these weeks trying to believe that he didn't even want her as a friend, now he was saying that he loved her. And looking into his face, she knew it was the truth. "I love Jesus, Dan. He is how I have managed to live through the last weeks." Dan was still watching her, hope a little stronger than fear now. But Hannah couldn't find words for anything else. She looked into his eyes, and they didn't need words anymore. He let his arms slip around her shoulders. Ever so slowly his lips touched hers, and time stood still for both of them.

A Letter To Our Readers

Dear Reader:

In order that we might better contribute to your reading enjoyment, we would appreciate your taking a few minutes to respond to the following questions. We welcome your comments and read each form and letter we receive. When completed, please return to the following:

Rebecca Germany, Fiction Editor
Heartsong Presents
PO Box 719
Uhrichsville, Ohio 44683

1. Did you enjoy reading *Some Trust in Horses?*
   ❑ Very much. I would like to see more books
      by this author!
   ❑ Moderately
      I would have enjoyed it more if _____

      _____

      _____

2. Are you a member of **Heartsong Presents**? Yes ❑ No ❑
   If no, where did you purchase this book? _____

   _____

3. How would you rate, on a scale from 1 (poor) to 5 (superior), the cover design? _____

4. On a scale from 1 (poor) to 10 (superior), please rate the following elements.

   _____ Heroine   _____ Plot

   _____ Hero   _____ Inspirational theme

   _____ Setting   _____ Secondary characters

5. These characters were special because_____

_____

_____

6. How has this book inspired your life?_____

_____

_____

7. What settings would you like to see covered in future
   Heartsong Presents books?_____

_____

_____

8. What are some inspirational themes you would like to see
   treated in future books?_____

_____

_____

9. Would you be interested in reading other **Heartsong
   Presents** titles?   Yes ❑   No ❑

10. Please check your age range:
    ❑ Under 18   ❑ 18-24   ❑ 25-34
    ❑ 35-45   ❑ 46-55   ❑ Over 55

11. How many hours per week do you read?_____

Name _____

Occupation _____

Address _____

City _____ State _____ Zip _____

Daily inspiration for Women

The apostle Peter wrote that a gentle spirit, not our outward appearance, is of great worth in God's sight. In our harsh and often heartless world, gentleness is a much-needed characteristic. With an emphasis on personal spiritual development, this daily devotional for women draws from the best writings of classic and contemporary Christian female authors.

384 pages, Printed Leatherette, 4 ³⁄₁₆" x 6 ³⁄₄"

❤ ❤ ❤ ❤ ❤ ❤ ❤ ❤ ❤ ❤ ❤ ❤ ❤ ❤ ❤ ❤ ❤

❤ ❤ ❤ ❤ ❤ ❤ ❤ ❤ ❤ ❤ ❤ ❤ ❤ ❤ ❤ ❤ ❤

·····Hearts♥ng·····

········Presents········

Heart♥ng Presents
Love Stories Are Rated G!

That's for godly, gratifying, and of course, great! If you love a thrilling love story, but don't appreciate the sordidness of some popular paperback romances, **Heartsong Presents** is for you. In fact, **Heartsong Presents** is the *only inspirational romance book club*, the only one featuring love stories where Christian faith is the primary ingredient in a marriage relationship.

Sign up today to receive your first set of four, never before published Christian romances. Send no money now; you will receive a bill with the first shipment. You may cancel at any time without obligation, and if you aren't completely satisfied with any selection, you may return the books for an immediate refund!

Imagine. . .four new romances every four weeks—two historical, two contemporary—with men and women like you who long to meet the one God has chosen as the love of their lives. . .all for the low price of $9.97 postpaid.

To join, simply complete the coupon below and mail to the address provided. **Heartsong Presents** romances are rated G for another reason: They'll arrive *Godspeed!*
